The Eddie Dickens Trilogy

Book One: A House Called Awful End
Book Two: Dreadful Acts
Book Three: Terrible Times

Unlikely Exploits

The First Unlikely Exploit: The Fall of Fergal
The Second Unlikely Exploit: Heir of Mystery

THE RISE OF THE

THE THIRD UNLIKELY EXPLOIT

HOUSE OF
MCNALLY

—or

*About
Time Too*

PHILIP ARDAGH

with illustrations by David Roberts

HENRY HOLT AND COMPANY | NEW YORK

~

In loving memory of Beanie,
put to sleep on March 27, 2003,
in her eighteenth year.
You were the bestest Bean there's ever been.

~

Henry Holt and Company, LLC
Publishers since 1866
115 West 18th Street
New York, New York 10011
www.henryholt.com

Henry Holt is a registered trademark of Henry Holt and Company, LLC
Text copyright © 2004 by Philip Ardagh
Illustrations copyright © 2004 by David Roberts
First published in the United States in 2005 by Henry Holt and Company
Originally published in Great Britain in 2004 by Faber and Faber Ltd.

Library of Congress Cataloging-in-Publication Data
Ardagh, Philip.
The rise of the house of McNally, or About time too / Philip Ardagh;
with illustrations by David Roberts.—1st American ed.
p.   cm.—(The third unlikely exploit)
Summary: In their third and final adventure, the McNally children meet Lionel Lyons,
who asks their help to fix problems that were created by time travelers.
ISBN-13: 978-0-8050-7478-9 / ISBN-10: 0-8050-7478-3
[1. Brothers and sisters—Fiction. 2. Space and time—Fiction. 3. Humorous stories.] I. Title:
Rise of the house of McNally. II. Title: About time too. III. Roberts, David, ill. IV. Title.
PZ7.A6776Ri 2005   [Fic]—dc22   2004054010

First American Edition—2005 / Designed by Meredith Pratt
Printed in the United States of America on acid-free paper. ∞
1   3   5   7   9   10   8   6   4   2

A Word to the Wise

There are those of you who were saddened by Fergal's death in *The Fall of Fergal*.

Now Fergal is back.

There are those of you who recoiled at yet more death in *Heir of Mystery*.

This should cheer you up.

There are those of you frustrated by not knowing what was causing the terrible outbreak of holes across the land.

Your frustration will soon be at an end.

There are those of you eager to find out the secret of Mr. Maggs's teddy bear.

The wait is over.

And as for Le Fay, Albie, and Josh's particular powers? Just give me time.

—Philip Ardagh

A fine wind is blowing the new direction of Time.

—D. H. Lawrence
From "Song of a Man Who Has Come Through"

PROLOGUE

Tick tock tick. . . . *Brrrrrrrrrrrrrrrrrrrrrrrrrrrrrr!*

Chapter One

There's a hastily assembled barricade in front of the door, made from a large filing cabinet pushed onto its side, a heavy table, a pile of chairs, and anything else they could lay their hands on: desk lamps, a water cooler, and even an empty fish tank. There are four of them making up the "they" in question. Carbonet is the smallest, and apart from his height—or lack of it—his most distinguishing feature (as it says on WANTED posters) is his hairy ears. I don't know if you've ever seen those little battery-operated gadgets designed for trimming nostril and ear hairs (they're often advertised in mail-order catalogs), but I suspect a whole drawer full of them wouldn't be enough to tackle his growth.

Next to Carbonet at this precise moment is Doyle. He looks a-bit-of-a-smoothy by nature, but deprived of a recent haircut and any hair oil, he looks less than at his best. He's looking forward to new clothes and a pampering . . . if they manage to escape.

Crouched down next to Doyle—and the only one who seems to be *doing* anything apart from worrying about being caught—is Smeek. Smeek is the tallest of them all and is most certainly the strangest looking. I'm not talking about his face. It's almost impossible to *see* his face. He has long straight jet-black hair (rather like an oversized hippie wig) growing down to his knees, and he has very spindly limbs.

Finally, there's Byron. What makes her stand out from the others is that she's a she. She's incredibly thin and has a permanent frightened rabbit-caught-in-the-headlights-of-an-oncoming-car expression on her face.

Until recently, one of the most frequently heard expressions in Byron's life has been: "Cheer up, it may never happen." Now, unfortunately, it *has* happened and Byron has every right to be looking scared half witless.

All four of them are wearing similar-looking slate gray jumpsuits (which presumably got their name from those suits parachutists wear when jumping out of airplanes). Each has their name stenciled in large black letters over their breast pocket: **CARBONET**, **DOYLE**, **BYRON**, and **SMEEK**. For some reason, Smeek has an additional X in square brackets after his name: **[X]**.

They're all barefoot and, by the state of their feet, have been for some time. Their soles have become hard skinned, toughened from walking without footwear, and, yes, they're more than a little grubby. Smeek appears to have five toes on one foot and seven on the other. In a way, it wouldn't look quite so strange if his twelve toes had been shared out evenly between the two.

The banging against the door is getting louder as someone on the other side, egged on by those around him, swings the metal cylinder of a fire extinguisher against the wood, causing the uppermost chairs on the barricade to teeter.

"Hurry, Smeek!" says Carbonet.

Smeek, who is using a red-handled screwdriver to tinker with a large piece of machinery in the middle of the room, simply grunts. He is holding a double-ended wrench in his mouth like a dog holding a bone. "I'm doing my best, old friend," he manages to mumble.

"Do you think this will work?" asks Byron, her voice all nervous and jumpy.

"It better," says Doyle, gently running his fingers through his collar-length hair. It's a nervous trait rather than a wish to look particularly handsome at this particular moment in time. "It's our only way out of—"

He's interrupted by a loud splintering noise as one of the door's panels splits apart.

"Time's running out," says Carbonet.

"This is hopeless!" wails Byron. (I'm sorry it's the only woman doing the wailing, but there it is.)

"I think we're ready," says Smeek. He stands back to admire his handiwork.

Imagine a giant car tire, or rubber ring, or ring doughnut but made from numerous pieces of metal held together with rivets and screws. Then imagine a tangle of wires trailing off to one side and a keypad—rather like one used for setting a burglar alarm or opening a door when you punch in a code—set at chest height on the right-hand edge of the ring. This is what's in the center of this room. This is what Smeek has been fine-tuning. The machine is humming now, like the overheated valves of an old radio, back in the days before transistors and microchips. (You'll have to take my word for it.)

"What if it doesn't work?" asks Byron.

"Then we're no worse off than if we didn't try it in the first place," Carbonet points out.

"We hope," mutters Doyle.

"WHAT?" demands Byron.

"No reflection on you, Smeek. I'm simply pointing out that this could be suicide," says Doyle.

"What are you saying?" asks Carbonet.

"He means that there's no guarantee that using the Doughnut will be safe," Byron jitters. She reaches into her breast pocket and pulls out a small mouse. "Which is why I must let you go, Kevin." She gently strokes the tiny rodent's head with trembling fingers. "I'll miss you." She gives the mouse a quick kiss, puts him on the floor, and he instinctively scurries for cover. With hindsight, this kindness will be a terrible mistake.

"It's a risk we're going to have to take," says Smeek. "We can only fit through one at a time. Who goes first?"

Someone has found a fire ax and is now using that on the door. It won't be long before their pursuers have made light work of their makeshift barricade and are on top of them.

"Let's stop talking and ACT!" says Doyle. He pushes in front of the others, and, before they can stop him, should they want to, he jumps through the hole in the middle of the Doughnut . . . and disappears.

"You next, Byron," says Carbonet.

"No, you."

Smeek takes Carbonet's hand. "Come on, old friend," he says. "We go together." He jumps through the Doughnut, pulling Carbonet after him. At that very moment, a number of things happen at once: the barricade gives way, a group of uniformed men spill into the room, and Kevin the mouse finishes chewing through one of the wires attached to the Doughnut, giving himself a nasty shock.

Seconds later, Byron jumps through the humming metal ring.

There is a loud FIZZ! followed by a bang, followed by silence. The humming has stopped. The machine is dead. Sadly, so is Kevin the mouse.

"They got away!" shouts one of the uniformed men.

"That's the least of our worries," says another, striding over to the Doughnut. "With the machine down we've lost their coordinates."

"What do we do?"

"Do? We tell no one, or . . ." He doesn't bother finishing the sentence. They all know how serious the situation has become. "Now let's get this mess cleared up." The room starts to rumble and shake.

The year is 1993. It is May 28, and the clock on the wall is edging toward three minutes past eleven, local time. In the seismology lab of the Zanger Institute Earthquake

Monitoring Station the needles of the earth-tremor recording equipment suddenly come to life, scribbling peaks and troughs across the graph paper like the lie detector readout of a babbling suspect or a medium frantically scrawling out "automatic writing," apparent messages from the spirit world.

Dougie—with an *ie*, not a *y*—is the scientist who's supposed to be monitoring the equipment, which usually means drinking plenty of coffee and doing crosswords and word-search puzzles. (Angie—also with an *ie*—who does the other shift, prefers logic puzzles and occasionally leaves her puzzle books lying around the lab. Dougie had a go at some of her logic puzzles once but just couldn't get his head around them.)

Now puzzles of any kind are banished from Dougie's thoughts. He sits bolt upright in his swivel chair, mutters "Strewth," turns to the keyboard of his computer, and frantically taps various keys. A zigzag line appears on a graph on his screen.

"Strewth," he says again, this time with even more feeling.

This is incredible. Somewhere in the Great Victoria Desert an earthquake or some kind of explosion or something has caused readings like nothing he's ever dreamed possible. Whatever's making the earth shake is well over *a hundred times* more violent than anything he's ever seen recorded for the region.

Dougie grabs the red phone, the one without buttons or a dial—like the ones you see very important people use in movies when they need a direct line to the president of the United States. "Hello?" he says. "Hello?"

"Hello," says a bleary voice at the other end.

"We have a Code Blue in the Great Victoria Desert," says Dougie, barely believing his own words.

"Code Blue?" says the voice.

"Code Blue," confirms Dougie.

"Strewth!" says the voice.

Over the next few days and weeks, scientists at the Zanger Institute will begin to try to piece together a picture of what occurred, combining results from scientific monitoring with eyewitness reports from people having seen what most of them describe as a "blinding flash of light in the sky" and earwitness reports from people having heard what most of them describe as "the loud boom of a distant explosion."

Zanger's experts, along with other experts from around the globe, will eventually rule out the possibility of an earthquake, a crashed meteorite, "something to do with UFOs," or even, as some will later claim, a secret and highly illegal underground test of a nuclear weapon developed by a Japanese terrorist group. The truth is that it's highly unlikely that they'll ever come up with the truth. Perhaps it's too incredible to believe. . . .

But happen it did, and you don't just have to take my word for it. It's history: May 28, 1993, near Banjawarn Sheep Station in the Great Victoria Desert, Western Australia.

.   .   .

"Is everyone okay?" asks Smeek, stumbling to his feet. He has a pounding headache and his hair has somehow become all tangled and full of sand. Sand? He looks around. It's a clear, dark night. Where on earth have they ended up? On a beach somewhere, perhaps? That'd be nice.

"Aoawpth!" says Doyle, spitting sand from his mouth. He's found himself facedown in the desert. He too has a headache like his worst ever hangover (and for those of you who've never drunk as much alcohol as Doyle, let me tell you that his worst ever hangover was *b-a-d*).

"Carbonet!" cries Smeek, running over to his small friend, who's lying, bleeding into the ground, the thirsty sand eagerly soaking up his blood. "He's badly hurt!" With the care of a father, Smeek gently lifts Carbonet's head.

"We made it?" asks Carbonet. "We got away?"

"We got away," nods Smeek.

"Where . . . when are we?"

Smeek forces a smile. "I've absolutely no idea whatsoever!" he confesses, surrounded by darkness.

"I hurt," says Carbonet.

"Where, old friend?"

"All over."

"Smeek!" Doyle groans from a short way off.

"What is it?" asks Smeek, carefully laying Carbonet's head back down on the ground, pushing some of the sand into a pile to make a pillow. Doyle calls out to him again. Smeek looks down at Carbonet. "I'll be back in a moment," he reassures him.

"Fine," says Carbonet forcing the words. "I'm not . . . not planning on going anywhere."

Smeek gets up and strides across the sand to Doyle. "What is it?" he whispers. "Carbonet is in a bad way and—" He stops and peers down at what Doyle is looking at through the blackness.

It's Byron . . .

. . . what's left of her. He can make out little more than a pile of blood-soaked clothes.

"Oh no . . . wh-wh-what have I done?" cries Smeek, falling to his knees. He buries his hair-hidden face in his hands. "What have I done?"

"She knew the risks," says Doyle, who's had time to prepare a response but still doesn't sound half as tough and heartless as when you read his words on the printed page.

"I don't understand . . . I don't understand . . . ," sobs Smeek, unaware, of course, that it was Byron's own pet mouse, Kevin, chewing through the wire that has caused the harm to her and Carbonet and was nothing he himself had done.

"Get up!" Doyle urges. "We've got to get moving. Who knows how long before someone works out exactly where to find us and follows us through the Doughnut." His head is pounding, pounding, pounding and he's finding it hard to focus his eyes, but the horrible death of Byron has helped him to focus his *mind* on the matter in hand.

"Carbonet is too badly hurt to move," Smeek says in a harsh whisper.

"But move him we must, Smeek," says Doyle, "or we could all end up dead."

Another time. Another place. Le Fay McNally is standing in a room. Much of it is in shadow. Something about the perspective seems a little strange: a little *off*. The walls don't quite meet the floor at right angles. The ceiling and the floor aren't quite parallel. Everything is in shades of gray. The window—yes, there's a window, though she hadn't noticed it before—is not quite square. It's as though she's on some arty set in a black-and-white movie, a cross between a Salvador Dali painting and a

1950s cartoon that exaggerates and distorts everyday objects.

In a corner stands the being Le Fay knows as Mr. Maggs, the being she saw fall to his inevitable death. His head is large, bald, and pumpkinlike. His teeth like shark's teeth. He looks up from whatever it is that he's doing.

"Who are you?" he asks in the familiar voice Le Fay thought that she'd never hear again.

"It's me, Le Fay McNally, Mr. Maggs," she says.

"What did you call me?" the being Le Fay knows as Mr. Maggs demands.

"Mr. Maggs," she repeats.

"And why do you call me that?"

"Because that's the name you insisted I call you," says Le Fay, stepping closer to him across the bare gray floorboards. "With the Mister and everything."

"When—?" begins Mr. Maggs. "Oh"—his expression changes—"I think I understand."

Since those unlikely events in Fishbone Forest, Le Fay has often wondered about his insistence on being called "Mister." Had he demanded the title so as to sound more human? Sure, he has two eyes, two arms, two legs, and just one head and nose, just as it should be—not too many, not too few—but put them all together, and you are left with something not quite so human after all.

"Mr. Maggs," says Mr. Maggs, slowly rolling the words around his mouth, as though trying out the name for size. He grins in the shadows. "I like that. . . . You say we've met?"

"Yes," Le Fay nods. "In Fishbone Forest. I was the girl looking—er—for her dog. Don't you remember? You had a fall. . . . We all thought you were dead."

"And what was I doing in this Fishbone Forest?"

"You were planning to implement your *Manifesto of Change*. . . ." Le Fay is really close to him now. There isn't a scratch on him. Not a bruise. Even if Mr. Maggs has somehow survived the fall—and she finds that very hard to believe—surely there'd be some sign of injury?

Mr. Maggs—and Le Fay has absolutely no doubt now that this is him—gives her an enormous grin. "A manifesto of change? What an excellent idea. Our meeting like this is most fortuitous, Le Fay McNally. Really most fortuitous . . ."

They're so close now that Le Fay can smell the familiar strange sweetness of his breath. Frightening though she finds Mr. Maggs, a part of her is glad that he survived. All he did was frighten them; he never did them any actual harm . . . though it's fair to say that if that big hole hadn't opened up beneath him, there's no way of knowing what he *might* have done.

"How did you get out?" she asks.

"Out?"

"Of the hole?"

"Mr. Maggs . . . Fishbone Forest . . . *Manifesto of Change* . . . the hole," says Mr. Maggs, as though all these names and concepts are somehow new to him, like unfamiliar items on someone else's shopping list. It's almost as if he's making no real connection with them.

Of course, thinks Le Fay. The fall. He must have hit his head in the fall down the hole. There must have been amnesia . . . loss of memory . . . cognitive deficits. (How can she, a young and poorly educated girl, know a phrase like that?) Then she notices how small Mr. Maggs now is. No, that's wrong. Compared to the other items in this strange and sparsely furnished room, Mr. Maggs is the same size he ever was; it's his size in comparison to *her* that has changed. She has become larger, which is why he looks smaller.

"I wish I understood what's happening," she says. "Everything is so strange."

Mr. Maggs—surely it really is Mr. Maggs, whatever he's calling himself now and whatever he does or doesn't remember?—is staring intently into her eyes.

"You work it out," he says.

Le Fay looks down to see what he was working on when she came into the room. Her eyes widen. She screams. If this were a dream, she'd wake up now.

But this isn't a dream.

Chapter Two

It's hot hot *hot* and the McNally children—though, of course, Jackie, the eldest, is actually an adult—are in Garland Park (which is rather a grand name for a not-so-grand area of mud and grass with a single tree roughly at its center). Like many places around town, it's named after the Garlands, a rich local family who used to own much of the land on which it's built. By far the richest local family, however, used to be the Lyonses. It was a Lyons who'd had Fishbone Forest planted and had Fishbone Hall built at its heart. The McNallys sometimes sit in the tree in Garland Park, but it's currently occupied by a whole gaggle of other kids, legs swinging from the branches under the shade of a "roof" made from a sheet of very rusty corrugated iron, the edges of which have given many a child a nasty deep cut over the years.

There's no room for the McNallys, but they don't seem too bothered by the heat anyway, except for Fergal with his shaggy dog's fur. His brothers and sisters like to throw sticks for him and he likes bringing them back, which you may think is weird what with him apparently having an ordinary boy's brain with an ordinary boy's thoughts. But the reasons are straightforward enough. First off, since occupying Bumbo the dog's body, Fergal has found that he has inherited a few doggy habits, and Bumbo must have been a big fan of fetching sticks. Secondly, it really is fun. He can't play most human games, but here's one he can get involved in with the others, and the twins in particular love the idea of getting their brother—yes, brother—to chase after sticks! Of course, with a "dog" who really does understand absolutely everything you say to him—rather than simply seeming to—they can develop some quite complicated rules too. Their antics often attract the attention of other dog owners, who make comments such as "Smart mutt" and "Boy, isn't he well trained!"

They're not playing stick games now, though. Too hot for Fergal. They're all sitting on the dry strawlike grass, patchy in the baked-mud earth, their backs up against part of the brick wall that has been built around a large hole that opened up in the ground one day last year— just one of the ever-increasing number of holes that have been appearing across the country. Though nowhere as big as some of the other holes, it's still far too deep for anyone to attempt to fill it in; hence the wall. Since the wall was built to replace the temporary barriers, a few foolish kids have walked around the top of it for a dare, but only a few. One slip or stumble and it really is a long way dow-ow-ow-ow-nnnnnnnn.

Life is good for the McNally family. With their father no longer drinking and his friendship with ex-naval and retired detective Charlie "Twinkle-Toes" Tweedy firmly cemented, wooden-legged Captain Rufus McNally is a happy man for the first time in years, and *his* happiness adds to that of Jackie, Le Fay, Albie, Josh, and Fergal. And then there's the computer Le Fay won in the Tap 'n' Type competition. With Fergal falling from their hotel window on the night of her victory, all thoughts of ever claiming the prize were forgotten . . . until Fergal came back to them, even if in four-legged form, that is. Since then, she and Jackie have gone and chosen the equipment, paid for it with the winning voucher, and then set it up in their apartment. It's by far the most valuable item in their home, and on more than one occasion, Le Fay's suggested they sell it, but Jackie—and later their dad, Cap'n Rufus—insisted that she'd earned it and she should keep it. It hasn't taken long for Le Fay to get to understand most of the programs and to show Albie and Josh how to play games on it, but she can't really use the computer quite as often as she'd like because they can't afford spending much on electricity. And she can't go online because the phone's been disconnected. But these are only minor hiccups in the grand scheme of things and not something she'd dream of ever telling the others.

Sometimes the McNallys still find themselves talking to each other about the events triggered by Le Fay getting to the finals of the competition. They discuss the hole that caused them to abandon the bus, meeting Mr. Peach the ventriloquist, Fergal's fall, and all those strange goings-on in Fishbone Forest. They wonder whatever happened to Mulch and the teenager Toby, but more often than not, the conversation returns to Mr. Maggs. What might have happened if that second hole hadn't swallowed him up? Would he really have tried to put his crazy *Manifesto of Change* into operation? Was he mad and bad? Both? Neither? He still seems to haunt their thoughts. Perhaps this is because he fell to his death, as Fergal had fallen, and they'd been helpless to help him.

"I wish we had money for an ice cream," says Josh.

"Me too," says Albie. "Just one between the four of us—"

Fergal barks.

"—the five of us," Albie corrects himself, "would be nice." (He doesn't really like sharing food and drink with Fergal. It usually comes back all slobbery.)

"Sorry, guys," says Jackie. "You know we can't afford it, but when I start my job, we should be able to splurge on a few luxuries." For years she's been responsible for look-ing after the others; it's not been something she's been able to trust her father to do. But now things are differ-ent. In the past she's been able to earn a little extra money doing a few odd jobs for other people from home—sewing, stuffing envelopes, making shuttlecocks (yes, making shuttlecocks), that kind of thing—but now she's got a job working at the SNAP-E-DREZZA clothing factory, less than an hour's walk from home. She's due to start in a couple of weeks.

"I wish we'd gotten that paper route," says Albie.

"Yeah," says Josh. "It's not fair that we have to have a bike." They'd tried arguing that they were used to walking, and, anyhow, there were two of them prepared to work together doing the one route for just one person's pay, but Mr. Ratsby, who organizes newspaper deliveries, was having none of it. "No bike, no job," he'd told them.

"I was wondering if we could get a job in a circus or on the stage or something," says Josh.

"What as? A pair of clowns?" grins Le Fay. Josh gives her a friendly punch on the shoulder. "Argh!" she says, deliberately overacting and rubbing her arm. "Bully! Picking on a poor defenseless girl!" This isn't a description any of them would use to describe their sister. Le Fay seems to have an ever-increasing sureness about everything she does nowadays. It's something that's hard to put into words.

"We were thinking that it might be useful for a magician—" begins Josh.

"—to have almost-identical twins—" continues Albie.

"—in his act," Joseph finishes. "The audience would think that we're the same person, which would make it a lot easier for the magician—"

"—to do some amazingly magical tricks."

"You've obviously given this a lot of thought," says Jackie, "but we live in a world where people like watching magicians with beautiful female assistants, wearing sparkly clothes with feathers in their hair."

"One look at your ugly mugs and they'd know there was something fishy going on!" says Le Fay. She's mocking herself as much as the twins because all three have the McNally red hair and gappy teeth. Jackie shares the red hair, but, in both jackal and human form, her teeth lack the McNally gap. Fergal used to have both gappy teeth *and* red hair . . . but now, of course, he's inherited Bumbo's and not the McNallys' genes.

Albie is about to say something, then stops. He leans forward, away from the wall, a puzzled expression on his face. He clutches his right arm with his left, holding it close to his chest. Suddenly, before their very eyes, his right arm—including his hand—swells up to an impossibly enormous size, then goes back to normal. In that brief moment, it's like Popeye's in the cartoons after he's swallowed a can of spinach and his arms bulge with incredibly exaggerated muscles. Imagine it: your arm ballooning out and growing in length, your hand becoming bigger than a strongman's. Then, seconds later, it's back to how it was before.

If this happened to one of our relatives, we'd either think we'd been imagining things, or we'd take him straight to the hospital. If it happened to us in person, we'd probably be thrown into a terrible state of panic. All five McNallys are shocked, all right, perhaps even a little frightened, and they know one thing for sure. Whatever just happened to Albie, it has to do with his secret power. Jackie, they know, can turn into a jackal. Whatever Fergal's power was going to turn out to be, it stopped his brain being splatted to nothing when his body had hit the pavement outside The Dell hotel. But Albie, Josh, and Le Fay's powers have yet to reveal themselves. Here is the very beginning, the first inkling, of what Albie's is going to be.

"What the—?" gasps Albie.

"Are you okay?" Josh asks his twin.

"Sure. Fine. . . . My arm's a little numb, that's all." He flexes his back-to-normal fingers on his back-to-normal hand at the end of his back-to-normal arm.

Jackie's already up on her feet. Le Fay's halfway there. "We're going to have to go home, NOW," says Jackie. "Who knows what might happen to you next."

"Do you think anyone saw?" asks Josh.

"If they did, they'll think they've caught heat stroke and are hallucinating," says Le Fay.

A short way off, by a trash can stuffed full of discarded drink bottles, cans, and ice-cream wrappers, a pair of eyes is watching them and has been for the past half hour or so, eyes belonging to someone who saw Albion McNally's fleeting transformation and doesn't doubt it for a single second.

Chapter Three

Malcolm Kent knocks on the huge mahogany door to the office of the chairman of Tap 'n' Type.

"Come!" says a voice.

Malcolm swings the door open and begins his walk across the acres of deep-pile gold-colored carpet toward Count Medoc Silverman's desk.

The desk is an extraordinary affair. Carved from one enormous piece of dark wood, it is covered in the most unusual carvings of vines and bears and wolves and hunters wearing antlered headdresses. You'd expect a Viking warrior to be seated behind such a threatening-looking piece of furniture. Instead, that position is occupied by Silverman, with his slicked-back hair, thin mustache, and perfect teeth. He is wearing one of his trademark pin-striped suits.

"Ah, Kent," he says with a welcoming smile. "Come in! Come in!" He glances at his chunky gold watch. "Thank you for being so prompt."

Malcolm has only ever been in the chairman's office on a couple of occasions, and the same thought strikes him this time as before. It seems strange that the man who has founded Tap 'n' Type, "Providers of Keyboards to the Crowned Heads of Europe & Beyond," doesn't have a single typewriter, word processor, or computer in his office. Count Medoc Silverman even writes company memos by hand, with one of his selection of gold fountain pens, in that distinctive red ink of his.

Count Silverman leans forward, placing his elbows on the large green blotter that takes up much of the top of his desk. "Forgive the cliché, but I expect you're wondering why I asked you here today, Malcolm."

"Indeed, Count," says Kent, who hasn't been thinking about much else all morning.

Count Silverman picks up the gold paper knife that he uses to slit open the tops of envelopes containing his private correspondence. The handle is as ornately carved as his desk. He runs the tip of the blade under his perfectly manicured fingernails. "It was a terrible thing when that brother of the Tap 'n' Type competition winner fell out of that window last year."

"Fergal McNally," says Malcolm, feeling a little put out that his boss appears not to remember the name. "It was awful, sir. Quite awful."

"And not the kind of publicity I intended the competition to generate."

"No," says Malcolm, taken aback.

"But accidents happen, and this was through no fault of your own. I felt the competition itself generated just the right buzz. You put the whole thing together very well."

"Thank you, Count. I've become a friend of the McNallys since then. They really are lovely peop—"

The count's eyes seem to open that little bit wider. "Of course we missed out on the damage limitation exercise of paying for a grand funeral. The hotel beat us to it on that one, I seem to recall. And didn't it rain? I imagine it was a washout."

Malcolm Kent looks down at his shoes sinking into the plush pile of the gold carpet. "The Dell paid for the coffin, if that's what you mean. . . ." He remembers the funeral clearly. Surprisingly, there'd been laughter as well as tears thanks to the twins' rubber ball. (You had to be there.)

Medoc Silverman stands up, looking every bit the slightly flashy used-car salesman that he isn't. He walks around his monstrosity of a desk to stand by Malcolm Kent. He puts his hand on his shoulder.

"But the past is the past, and I've asked you here to talk about your future. I'm promoting you to publicity director, effective immediately." He grasps Malcolm Kent by the hand and shakes it. "Congratulations," says the count.

"Th-thank you, sir," says a somewhat surprised Malcolm.

"We must toast your success." Silverman walks over to a wall unit and pulls down a flap to reveal a row of bottles of red wine. He selects one, handing it to Malcolm along with a gold corkscrew. "Perhaps you would do the honors?"

"Er, thank you," says Malcolm.

As Malcolm uncorks the bottle and Count Medoc Silverman places two large wineglasses on his blotter, Malcolm reflects that, despite the name *Silver*man, the count seems to much prefer gold. His cuff links, his watch, his ring, his fountain pens, his corkscrew, even the color of his carpet? All gold! On the walls of his office are mounted various musical instruments—a saxophone, a trumpet, a flute, a trombone, and a tuba—and they too are made of gold.

The bottle open, Count Medoc Silverman half fills the two glasses, handing one to Malcolm Kent and raising the other himself. "To your promotion," he says. The two men drink. Malcolm thinks the wine tastes delicious. "Do sit," says Silverman, going back to his side of the desk.

Malcolm looks around. There appears to be nowhere *to* sit. "Thank you, I prefer to stand," he says, which is probably the best answer to give when there are no other chairs in a room.

"I insist," says Medoc. "Use that ugly elephant thingy as a stool." He points in the direction of a small elephant carving beneath the large window that lets the brilliant sunlight into his office, showing the thousands of usually unseen dust particles floating in the air.

Malcolm strides over to the elephant, carrying it back to the front of the chairman's desk, then squats on it. His position reminds him of a picture he once saw of Puddleglum the Marshwiggle in a book called *The Silver Chair*. He feels that he's all knees and feet.

They drink.

"There are exciting times ahead," says Silverman.

Later that same afternoon, Count Medoc Silverman stares up at the ceiling, deep in thought, listening to jazz on the office sound system, when there is a tap-tap-tapping. It isn't coming from the door to his outer office but from the door leading to his private staircase down to his private garage beneath the Tap 'n' Type building. The door with the lucky gold horseshoe on it.

He frowns. "Who is it?" he hisses.

"Duffel," says a muffled voice.

The count jumps up out of his chair and over to the door, yanking it open. There in front of him stands an oversized teddy bear, his thread unraveling in places and looking very grubby indeed. You wouldn't look too great either if you'd had to crawl your way out of a huge hole and had been sleeping rough ever since. For here is Mr. Maggs's onetime constant companion.

The count is silent for what seems like an age. "How on earth did you find me?" he gasps at last.

"It was only a matter of time," says the teddy bear, fixing him with a glassy stare. "You may have changed your name, but you haven't lost your flair for publicity." He pads across the plush carpet, leaving a slightly sooty trail.

"Where's . . ." Medoc pauses whilst he remembers the name. "Mr. Maggs? I thought you two arc supposed to be inseparable."

Duffel puts his paws on the seat of the count's chair and then clambers up into it. "Dead," he says.

The count switches off the jazz. Silence. "When? How?" he asks eventually.

"Last winter. I can't remember exactly," says Duffel. "I've lost track of time." At the mention of the word *time* he lets out a strange laugh. Come to think of it, any kind of laugh from a teddy bear would be strange. Generally they don't laugh . . . or walk . . . or talk. Then again, Duffel isn't like other bears. "We fell. He didn't stand a chance. Luckily for me I have all this padding . . . and," he adds quietly, "I landed on top of him. He cushioned my fall. That's what I'm here about. The rips—"

There is a knock at the main door to the office, and, before the count has time to say anything, his secretary,

Miss Willis, strides into the room. She immediately sees the grubby teddy bear on Count Silverman's chair.

"H-how sweet, Count," she says politely.

Count Silverman picks up Duffel and hugs him to his pin-striped jacket. "An old family heirloom," he smiles. "It's been a much-loved member of the family for many a year."

He opens a bottom drawer of his huge desk, places Duffel inside it, and slides it shut.

"Just a few letters requiring your signature, Count," says Miss Willis, placing them on the count's blotter and unscrewing the lid of one of his many gold fountain pens for him. "And you asked me to remind you that you plan to tour the factory at three-thirty." She hands him the pen.

"Thank you, Miss Willis," says Medoc, signing each letter with a flourish of red ink and turning it over to dry on the blotter.

Miss Willis leaves the room.

There is a banging coming from the bottom of Count Medoc Silverman's desk.

"Let me out of here!" comes a muffled cry.

For the time being, Silverman leaves him where he is.

Chapter Four

As the chairman of Tap 'n' Type makes his way down his private staircase to his private garage beneath his office building, he has Duffel tucked under his arm. It is unlikely he'll run into anyone as he makes his way to his gold-plated Bentley—that's a car, and a rather nice one at that—but he isn't going to take any chances. It would look strange enough, him carrying a battered oversized teddy bear, but a teddy bear running alongside him would have been pretty much impossible for him to explain away!

"And don't say a word," Silverman insists before scooping Duffel up out of the drawer and wedging him under his armpit.

Duffel does as he is told. He is used to keeping his mouth shut after years with Mr. Maggs. He'd never spoken when anyone else was around and had had to be careful even when there wasn't. With so many holes in the walls and missing doors at Fishbone Hall, where they'd lived, they could never be sure who might overhear them.

Duffel is also used to seeing the world from a teddy bear's angle. Picked up and plonked down here, there, and everywhere.

Once Duffel is in the front passenger seat and Medoc Silverman in the driver's, he feels that it's okay to break his silence.

"I should have known that you'd do the best out of all of us," Duffel says as the Bentley drives up the ramp and out of the underground garage into the brilliant sunshine. "You always were the smart one."

Medoc Silverman keeps his eyes on the road in front. "And, in this time and this place, my name is Count Medoc Silverman, and I'll thank you to remember that."

"If you say so," says Duffel. He looks at Silverman with his neatly slicked-down hair, his perfectly pampered mustache, and his expensive (but rather flashy-looking) clothes. "Is Medoc Silverman a real person whose identity you borrowed . . . or did you make him up?"

Medoc Silverman eases the gold-plated Bentley to a halt at an intersection. The traffic light is red. He turns to face the teddy bear. "You spent too much time with Maggs," he says, his voice even, yet somehow menacing. "He was the evil genius—"

"There was nothing evil about him. He was just misunderstood—" Duffel protests, but the count ignores him.

"Well, whatever he was, he was the one with the big schemes. I, on the other hand, went down the simpler hard-work route and am now a highly successful businessman. Tap 'n' Type is a well-respected company providing an excellent service across the globe. I didn't need to steal anyone's identity. I created Count Medoc Silverman out of nothing."

"Don't you think that blending into the background might have been safer?" asks Duffel.

The traffic light changes to green, and Medoc Silverman drives the car across the intersection. "I can't believe I'm hearing that from a talking teddy bear!" he laughs.

Duffel puts a paw on Silverman's arm and stares at him with his glassy teddy-bear eyes. The chairman of Tap 'n' Type looks down at him in his plush leather seat.

"I have no choice," he says quietly. "That is what I have become."

"I know," says Silverman, his tone gentler now. "I'm sorry. I shouldn't have said that . . . but why shouldn't I have a new name and a new lifestyle and all the very public trappings of success that go with it? I created Count Medoc Silverman, founded Tap 'n' Type, and built it up into the success it is today. And I want to enjoy that success. We all got a second chance and I've grabbed it with both hands."

Duffel looks down at his own threadbare paws. "Some guys have all the luck," he mutters.

The Bentley reaches a stretch of open road. "I'm happy to help you, Duffel," says Silverman. "Happy to feed you and . . . er . . . ." He is about to add "and clothe you," but it occurs to him that he isn't sure whether teddy bears generally wear clothes or not. ". . . er . . . give you some

money, but I can't risk your being around. The past is the past. We have to look to the future."

Duffel makes a strange noise. It is the teddy-bear equivalent of an indignant snort. "We all know what the future has to offer," he says. "That's what got me into this mess."

Silverman says nothing; he simply pulls the car into the fast lane and puts his foot right down on the accelerator.

Tick tock. Time to move. Forward. Sideways. Backward. Time ticks on. Time for a thought or two. Or three. Ready? *At the time it happens, every moment in history takes place in the present.* Hmmm. *The very latest craze is only the very latest craze until the next very latest craze comes along.* Mmmm. *Today's baby is tomorrow's grandparent.* Have a banana.

It's a beautifully clear silvery moonlit evening. There are few people about, and Jackie and Fergal are chasing each other back and forth across a local playing field. Jackie is in jackal form and so can communicate with her doggy brother without spoken words. They're "talking" as they run, chase, and play.

JACKIE: *Are you happy?*

FERGAL: *Happier than I've ever been, Jacks. If only we could explain to the others what it's like to run on four legs and to feel the wind in your fur.*

JACKIE: *Ouch!*

FERGAL: *And to be able to nip your big sister's tail!*

JACKIE: *And the smells. What about the smells?*

Fergal stops and lifts his leg against a tree. He can't help it. There'll always be a little bit of Bumbo in his behavior.

FERGAL: *I'm still having to get used to them. I never knew that everything smelled so strong through a dog's nose!*

They chase each other around and around and in and out of a small clump of trees at the edge of the field.

Suddenly an elderly man crosses their path. His skin looks blue in the moonlight.

FERGAL: *!?!*

JACKIE: *What's wrong?*

FERGAL: *It's him. . . .*

JACKIE: *Who?*

FERGAL: *The man from Fishbone Forest . . .*
JACKIE: *WHO?*
FERGAL: *Lionel Lyons!*
JACKIE: *Who?*
FERGAL: *Lionel Lyons! Well . . . it's his body.*
JACKIE: *You mean . . . ?*

Jackie and Fergal stand stock-still. The old man bends down and pats Fergal on the head.

"It *is* you!" he says, with obvious pleasure, studying the scar in Bumbo's head where Mulch had cut it open. "So you survived the scalpel too, did you, boy?"

Jackie is intrigued. Here is a man who can not only tell them more of what went on last winter in Fishbone Hall before she and the others arrived on the scene—Fergal's recollection is patchy and he spent much of the time locked up in an outbuilding anyway—but he's also probably the only person Fergal will ever get to meet who shares the almost unique experience of being a brain in someone else's body. Dashing behind a tree, Jackie turns back into human form and slips into her clothes, which she's left neatly folded on the grass. She emerges in the moonlight.

"Hello," she says to the man in Lionel Lyons's body.

"Oh, hello," he says. Fergal bounds over to Jackie. "Is he your dog?"

Jackie nods.

"Just the one?" he asks. "He was playing with another very handsome beast a moment ago." His voice sounds old but not frail. In the same way that Fergal speaks with Bumbo's bark, this man must sound a lot like Lionel Lyons used to.

Jackie glows with inner pride. She's never been called a handsome beast before. "Just Fergal," she says, bending down and giving her brother a good solid pat. "You're Lionel Lyons, aren't you?" she adds.

The man is visibly surprised. "You . . . you must be mistaken," he says.

"Technically, I suppose," says Jackie. "I mean, all your thoughts and feelings aren't Mr. Lyons's, but you are in his body, aren't you?"

"I—er—" The man who had his brain placed in Mr. Lyons's body—he was a French teacher, wasn't he?— actually splutters.

"There's so much I want to ask you," says Jackie. Fergal is jumping up, barking at his big sister, but, because she's now in human form, she can't understand him. But *he* can understand her. "Shall I tell him?" she asks. Fergal nods. Jackie looks up at the man. "I was at Fishbone Forest. I met Mr. Maggs, Mulch, and Toby. I know about the Lyons fortune and your brain being put in that body." She pauses. "You're not alone. This," she says, looking back down at Fergal, "is my brother."

For the first time in this brief encounter, the man looks really, *really* surprised. He may even have turned a funny color, but it's hard to tell in the moonlight.

Let's fast-forward. Just a little. Not too far. Stop! Back a bit. Great! Here's fine. We're back at the McNallys' apartment with Smoky the cat in the "nest" she's made for herself on top of the wardrobe in the bedroom.

In the front room, all the McNallys are assembled, including their father, Captain Rufus, who is the only McNally sitting in an actual chair. Perched on one of its arms is Albie and on the other is Josh. The two remaining chairs are occupied by the French teacher inside Lionel Lyons's body and Mr. Charlie "Twinkle-Toes" Tweedy, the retired police detective who was paying one of his regular visits to the apartment when Jackie and Fergal turned up with their surprise guest.

Le Fay was using her computer when they arrived. The twins were in bed. Now they're all very wide awake indeed and giving the newcomer their undivided attention. Le Fay is sitting on a windowsill, the moonlight filtering through the grubby glass, with Fergal curled up at her feet, whilst Jackie—who is very much in charge of these proceedings—is sitting on a very large (and very lumpy) homemade cushion opposite their guest.

"Please tell the others what you started telling me on the way over," says Jackie.

The ancient gentleman—well, that's what he is on the *outside*, at least—looks around the assembled company. "My name is Tom Dwyer," he says, sounding a little nervous, "and I used to teach French in a truly terrible school in Hartingly called Gravel Hall . . . where the only thing worse than the students was their parents. It was a horrible, horrible job." He takes a sip of tea.

Despite Twinkle-Toes Tweedy helping Cap'n Rufus get all the benefits he's entitled to, money is still tight in the McNally household and, except on very special occasions, tea bags get used time and time again, until the last trace of tea color has gone. (Flavor has very little to do with it.)

What none of them knows is just *how* special their meeting with Tom Dwyer (in Lionel Lyons's body) will turn out to be.

"I hated teaching. I hated my home life," Dwyer explains. "My parents died when I was little and I was brought up by an aunt who fed me and cared for me and always tried to do what was right for me, but she never knew how to show her *love* for me, if she actually felt any."

Albie and Josh watch him speak with fascination. They remember Mr. Maggs talking about his hare-brained scheme in which he'd needed the dead Lionel Lyons to make "one final appearance" so that Mr. Maggs could be made heir to the Lyons fortune and now here he is. Here is Mr. Lyons's body with another man's brain inside his head, of course . . . living and breathing (and drinking tea-colored water) in front of them. It's weird enough having a brother who's now a dog, but imagine if he'd come back looking and sounding like a completely different *person*. In a way that might have been even harder to cope with.

"When I left home, I went to France for a few years. I didn't like it . . . ," Dwyer continues.

Le Fay begins to wonder whether the French teacher has ever liked *anything* much!

". . . so I came home and taught the language. I wasn't much qualified for anything else." He finishes his tea and places the mug on the arm of his chair, next to a hole where the stuffing is poking through the cover. "I never married. I never even had a girlfriend."

Fergal is studying the newcomer more intently than anyone else in that room. Of all those present, only Fergal really knows what it's like for Tom Dwyer's thoughts, ideas, reactions—his very *being*—to be occupying a different body, a body that was once occupied by someone else . . . by someone else who has died and vacated it. Both he and the French teacher are new tenants in old properties left empty when their previous occupants moved on.

"My last memory as Tom Dwyer in my original body was down by the docks. I fell in the water. Perhaps I jumped. . . . I'm not altogether sure. I remember fighting for breath . . . drowning . . . then I was hit by a boat . . . and then the next thing I remember clearly is waking up in what seemed like a hospital room with a teenage boy and a—er—man clutching a teddy bear. . . . I was confused. . . . Then I saw my hands. . . . They didn't seem to belong to me. . . . It was like a nightmare."

Charlie "Twinkle-Toes" Tweedy produces a small metal flask from the hip pocket of his checked jacket and pours a splash of something into Dwyer's empty tea mug.

"Have a sip of this," he says. "It'll do you a power of good."

Captain Rufus McNally raises a quizzical eyebrow. He's never seen Twinkle-Toes produce his hip flask before and has never touched a drop of alcohol himself since he first learned of Fergal's fall.

Dwyer swallows the drink gratefully, then resumes his incredible tale. "It took time to adjust to my new body and my new surroundings, but, as it transpired, I was Mr. Maggs's pet project and he went out of his way to make sure that I adapted and was comfortable—"

"So long as you did exactly what he said."

The man inside Mr. Lyons's old body nods. "He told me that he and Lionel Lyons had been old friends and that having no family left, Lionel had intended to write a will leaving everything to him, but that sadly, Lionel had died before he'd had the chance to do it."

Which was almost the truth, Le Fay thinks. In fact, by his own admission, Mr. Maggs had deliberately befriended the old man with the sole purpose of trying to persuade him to leave him the Lyons family fortune.

"He explained that he needed me to play the part of Lionel—and argued that the flesh and bone part of me really *was* Lionel anyway—and that I must visit Mr. Fudge of the lawyers Garland & Fudge and write a will making Mr. Maggs sole beneficiary—which I did."

"Did he threaten you? Say what would happen if you didn't go along with this extraordinary state of affairs?" asks Twinkle-Toes Tweedy, his detective instincts coming to the fore.

Dwyer shakes the head he's come to think of as his own. "No. He pointed out that he'd given me back my life . . . and in return, all he wanted was this one small favor. Little did he know how little I valued his gift at first. . . ."

Albie and Josh look at each other from the separate arms of their father's chair. Tom Dwyer certainly isn't a bundle of laughs.

The "cheer up, it might never happen" line would be rather wasted on him too, I suspect. And phrases, such as "Let's do it for the fun of it," "Just for a laugh," and, "Hey, let's party," are unlikely to roll off his tongue, which, given what he's been through, is understandable, I suppose.

"Of course, it took me a while to realize the other implication in Mr. Maggs's plan as he presented it to me. Writing a will wasn't *all* he needed from me. There was more. Much more." Dwyer pauses, looking at his old, gnarled hand clutching the mug on the arm of the chair. "As Lionel Lyons, I went with Mr. Maggs to the offices of Garland & Fudge, met with old Mr. Fudge, and said all the things that Mr. Maggs had coached me to say. I had them draw up a will leaving everything to Mr. Maggs, just as he wanted. But . . ." He trails off into silence.

"But of course!" cries Le Fay, with a look of horror. "For Mr. Maggs to inherit the Lyons fortune, *you had to die first!*"

Chapter Five

There is a loud gasp in the McNallys' sparsely furnished front room, made up from all the barely audible sharp intakes of breath coming from each and every one of them, except for Charles "Twinkle-Toes" Tweedy, whose years as a detective have trained him to hide his emotions, and for Fergal, who lets out a puppylike yelp instead.

"When did it occur to you that you were going to be required to—er—die?" asks Tweedy, leaning right forward in his chair, reminding Le Fay of a bird of prey on the lookout for a passing mouse.

"It didn't," confesses Dwyer. "I was still trying to adjust to the fact that I was alive again and, in one sense, was someone else. Then there was the fact that I was more or less a prisoner in a semi-derelict house in the heart of some godforsaken forest in one of the wettest winters on record. It was his assistant, Mulch—Jackie says you children met him—who warned me."

Fergal's ears are twitching at the mention of Mulch, the nickname of one Stefan Multachan, petty crook, assistant to the late Mr. Maggs, and a skilled surgeon in his own right. He was the one who'd put Fergal's brain in Bumbo's body.

Le Fay's legs are going numb from being perched half on and half off the windowsill. She stands up and steps over Fergal, who is having a good old scratch behind his left ear with a hind leg (something not all brothers can do).

"But I don't get it, Mr. Dwyer. When we had the misfortune to meet Mr. Maggs, his plan was complete. The way he told it, he'd *already* inherited the millions. He claimed that he was the owner of Fishbone Hall and was ready to spend some of the fortune to make his *Manifesto of Change* come true! But you're still alive."

"Yes," says Albie.

"How come?" asks Josh.

"Thanks to Mulch," says Dwyer. "He not only pointed out the less-pleasant aspect of Mr. Maggs's plan but also helped me to escape."

RRRRRRRRRRRRRRRRRRewind.

"We've got to get you out of here," says Mulch, the rain dripping from his plastic raincoat onto the already sodden and warped floorboards.

"I thought I'd done everything your Mr. Maggs had asked of me," says Dwyer, looking up from his chair.

"There's no time to argue," Mulch insists. "The master could be back at any moment. Here. Put this on." He throws a shabby raincoat into Dwyer's lap.

Dwyer gets to his feet, feet that once belonged to Lionel Lyons, mind and body. "You mean Mr. Maggs doesn't know you're moving me?"

"No," says Mulch with added urgency. *"Pleeease!* We must hurry."

Pulling on the raincoat as he walks, he follows Mulch through various holes in the crumbling walls of Fishbone Hall and down a flight of back stairs. Outside in the terrible rain now, they pass an outbuilding, triggering off a spate of excited barking from within.

"Sssh!" hisses Mulch. "That stupid dog is going to give us away!" He and Dwyer clamber into Mulch's English-mustard-colored van.

"You love that dog," says Dwyer, pulling the seat belt across the late Lionel Lyons's body, which he's already beginning to think of as his own. "I've seen you nurse him and play with him. Since Mr. Maggs—er—brought me back, that's the only love I've seen in this horrible place. You and that boy Toby seem to obey your so-called master out of fear and there's no love lost between the pair of you."

The little van is speeding down the driveway, heading between spiny trees, windshield wipers frantically sweeping back and forth, back and forth, trying to cope with the ceaseless rain.

"You're forgetting Mr. Maggs and Duffel," says Mulch, craning forward over the steering wheel to try to see his way through the downpour.

"You mean that there's more than the four of us in that crumbling excuse for a house?"

"Five, if you count the dog," says Mulch.

Dwyer counts off the occupants on the fingers of one of his new (secondhand) hands: "You, me, Mr. Maggs, Toby, and the dog makes five. Then who's Duffel?"

"The master's teddy bear."

Dwyer snorts. "Yes, I'll grant you that. He certainly seems to love his bear."

Mulch swerves the van around a bend a little too sharply and almost loses control of the vehicle.

"Careful!" says Dwyer. "I don't want to end up dead again so soon—"

"Which is why I must get you away from here," says Mulch, sweat breaking out on his brow, which is already splattered with rain.

"W-why?"

"For Mr. Maggs to inherit the Lyons billions, he needs a death certificate, and for him to get a death certificate, he needs—"

"A body."

Mulch nods.

Tom Dwyer, ex-teacher of French, sits in silence as the little van the color of English mustard speeds toward one of the exits of Fishbone Forest.

Back at the hall, there is a knock on Mr. Maggs's study door. "Come!" he says.

Toby the teenager ambles in, the headphones to his Discman around his neck. His T-shirt reads DON'T SHOOT ME, I JUST WORK HERE.

Mr. Maggs is standing by a window, one that isn't simply a hole in an outer wall but has a frame and glass and everything. The effect of normality is slightly spoiled by ivy growing across it *from the inside.*

Duffel is leaned against the wall beneath it.

"Well?" demands Mr. Maggs.

"Mulch has just smuggled the patient out of the house," Toby reports.

A satisfied smile spreads across Mr. Maggs's extraordinarily wide face. "Oh, goody!" he says. "I want you to buy me a bunch of plastic tulips."

"What's that got to do—?"

"All you need to know is that I want a bunch of plastic tulips. What it has or hasn't to do with is my affair!"

Mr. Maggs is struggling not to fly into a terrible rage. He doesn't want to. He doesn't need to. He must simply impart his orders to the boy as coolly and calmly as possible. But there's that telltale tremble in his voice.

"Sorry. . . . Yes. Of course . . . ," Toby mumbles.

"Yes?" Mr. Maggs pauses.

"Yes, *master*," Toby adds hurriedly.

Mr. Maggs bends down, picks up his teddy bear, and holds him tight. "If this all goes according to plan, Toby—and it *will* go according to plan—I will soon inherit this house, this forest, and all that lovely money and I shall be able to implement my *Manifesto of Change* . . . and you, Toby, shall be richly rewarded for your loyalty. Remember that. Richly rewarded."

"I'll remember," Toby assures him. To him, cash and lots of it is what this is all about.

"In the meantime, first thing tomorrow morning you will take what money you need from the kitty in the egg-bowl in the kitchen, go into town, and *buy me some plastic tulips.*" These last few words are spoken through two rows of pointy little teeth, clenched together.

"Thy will be done," Toby intones, without a trace of irony. He leaves Mr. Maggs to his thoughts, closing the door quietly behind him.

"There's nothing like discovering that someone else is planning to take your life away to make you want to keep it!" Dwyer tells the assembled McNallys. "Mulch took a big risk helping me. A big risk."

Fergal stops scratching and barks his approval. He's a big Mulch fan.

"Have you any idea how Mr. Maggs ended up inheriting Lionel Lyons's wealth without a body?" asks Twinkle-Toes Tweedy.

"Oh, yes," says Dwyer. "According to Mulch, he managed to acquire a death certificate by unscrupulous means."

"He forged one?"

"I think it involved a genuine doctor signing a genuine certificate," Dwyer explains, "but how Mr. Maggs got him to sign it is another matter. Mulch was very hazy on the subject."

"Which means you've seen him since he helped you escape?"

"In fact, you still see him, don't you?" says Le Fay. It sounds like a challenge to deny it. "In fact, it was he who told you that you might find Fergal and—er—another dog chasing each other up on the playing field. What you didn't expect was for us to recognize *you*. You didn't run into Jackie by coincidence, did you?"

"Y-yes," confesses Tom Dwyer. "I mean no. No, I didn't. I do still see him. . . . How did you know?"

"She has brains," says Albie, which is an unfortunate choice of words, given who he's talking to.

"Not in jars," Josh adds helpfully.

Le Fay frowns. How did she know? How does she know so many of the things that suddenly seem to be competing for space in her mind nowadays? She shrugs. "I just worked it out," she says.

ChapTeR SiX

The following morning, Tom Dwyer returns to the McNallys' apartment and takes Jackie, Le Fay, Fergal, and the twins to see Mulch. Their father wants Twinkle-Toes Tweedy to go too but, as an adult herself, Jackie assures him that the children have nothing to fear.

They walk. It's not far and, anyway, the McNallys certainly can't afford to take the bus. Fergal keeps bounding excitedly ahead, his long pink tongue lolling in the morning heat. He's very much looking forward to seeing Mulch again, but the others aren't quite so sure.

It turns out that all this time Tom Dwyer has been living in an apartment less than three-quarters of an hour's walk from the McNallys' home! (Three-quarters of an hour if they were striking out on their own, that is. This particular trip takes well over an hour because Tom Dwyer is in the body of a very old man, remember.)

"This was where Mulch brought me the night he drove me away from Fishbone Hall," Dwyer explains as they walk across the lobby toward the elevator.

"No dogs," says a security guard seated behind a small counter.

The twins are impressed. All they can see of him is the dome of his head poking up above the top of the large newspaper he's reading and his feet, which he has up on the counter . . . and if that's all they can see of him, how did he manage to spot Fergal (who didn't make a single yap, bark, or whimper)?

"We haven't got a dog," says Le Fay, frantically signaling Fergal to hide before the man lowers his paper.

Fergal darts behind a large square plant pot made of the same pinkish simulated marble as the foyer floor. This probably makes the entrance to the apartments sound far grander than it really is. Of course, this is far grander than the building the McNallys' apartment's in, but that's not saying much. The Garland Apartment Building, which is where they are now, was probably once far grander. The old phrase "It's seen better days" seems very apt. The floor has lost its luster and the plant pot, behind which Fergal is now hidden, is badly cracked and contains a plastic pretend plant that hasn't been dusted since the day it was placed there.

The security guard pulls his feet off the counter and folds his paper as he stands up.

"Don't mess with me, lady," he says. "These ears ain't ever been wrong." His accent sounds strange.

"Are you an American?" asks Le Fay because, don't forget, whichever country you think this story is taking place in, you're W-R-O-N-G.

"I surely am," says the guard, who, incidentally, is called Arthur P. Peabody III. The Roman numeral "III" after his name means that he is the third Peabody to have been given the name Arthur P. Peabody, so the correct way to address him—and I don't mean you to confuse him with an envelope or a package—would be as Arthur P. Peabody the Third . . . which is probably more in keeping with the name of a senior vice president of a multiglobal sock-making company or a software giant, whatever a software giant may be, than with a security guard in what he himself once described as "a two-bit flea pit of a building."

"I've always wanted to go to America," says Le Fay. Fergal's tail is sticking out behind the plant pot, and she's trying to push it out of sight with her foot whilst keeping her eyes firmly fixed on Mr. Peabody.

"I strongly suspect that you're trying to change the subject," declares Peabody. "I believe we was discussing the fact that I distinctly heard the pitter-patter of doggy paws on my marble floor."

"Well—" begins Le Fay, relieved to see out of the corner of her eye that Fergal has pulled his tail in.

"The clackety-click of claws on marble floors—"

"You're a poet!" Albie grins.

"—like little knitting needles," continues the security guard, ignoring the boy.

"Well—" says Le Fay.

"Good morning, Arthur!" Tom Dwyer interrupts. "I've got a little something for you." He shuffles across the foyer, digging his hand into the pocket of his lightweight summer jacket, already a little damp with sweat from having caught a cab to the McNallys' and then walking back with them.

"Oh, really, Mr. Smith—" says Peabody, because that's the name the kindly old gentleman gave him when he moved in. (It would have been extremely unwise to refer to himself as either Dwyer or Lyons, now, wouldn't it?) Dwyer produces a small lozenge-shaped can of pilchards in tomato sauce and places it on the counter by the folded-up newspaper. "—You shouldn't have." Peabody slips the can out of sight. "I'm sure I must have imagined those doggy sounds. My hearing ain't quite what it used to be. My ears must have been hallucinatin' again."

The others aren't quite sure whether ears really *can* hallucinate, but they get his meaning. Arthur P. Peabody III sits back down, unfolds his paper, and puts it up as a screen between himself and the elevator. He's already looking forward to his lunchtime pilchard sandwich. He has a loaf and a sharp knife in his cubbyhole. In this weather, there's no point in bringing any butter, margarine, or even that low-fat spread his wife (Alice Peabody) would far rather he ate. It would melt in minutes, and the management of the Garland Apartment Building is too cheap to provide him with a fridge. Not even a small one. Which is why Mr. Peabody's bottles of beer are annoyingly warm in their hidey-hole under the counter. Peabody sighs a silent sigh to himself—an inner sigh—and ruminates on the fact that life is, in his opinion, not always very fair. (It may have occurred to you that this is not a particularly original thought, but at least it's true.)

Tom Dwyer and the McNallys meanwhile are taking advantage of the window of opportunity the bribe has afforded them. In other words, they all nip into the elevator, Fergal included, before the security guard changes his mind, Fergal's paws clackety-clacking those last few steps across the foyer.

"My ears never lie," Peabody can be heard to mutter.

Up in Mulch and Dwyer's apartment, the McNallys recognize some of the items dotted about the place. Mulch must have brought them from Fishbone Hall after

Mr. Maggs fell to his death. Of course, his book—his *Manifesto of Change*—has been lost. Jackie had thrown it into the hole after him.

Dwyer makes them all sit down before Mulch makes his entrance. Jackie can clearly recall the time she last saw him.

It is raining. Still raining. It's hard to remember when it *hasn't* been raining. Jackie's heart feels like bursting with joy. Looking into the eyes of the dog sitting on Le Fay's lap and being petted by the twins, she knows that Fergal is well and truly back.

She looks up and—through a large hole in the ceiling above and a large gap in the roof of the room above *that*—can clearly see the sky, splashes of falling rain mixing with the tears on her face.

"We did it, Mum," she whispers. "Thank you."

She looks down to see Mulch kneeling by the hole in the floor of Fishbone Hall into which his master has fallen. The earth smells rich and damp. He is sobbing gently.

A pang of guilt stabs Jackie, but it's quickly replaced with one of confusion and anger. But what harm has Mulch done them? Not a lot. Mulch has brought Fergal back to them. She puts her hand on his shoulder. He looks up at her with such sadness.

"He wasn't a bad man," he says for the umpteenth time.

"Maybe not *all* bad," Jackie concedes.

Mulch gets to his feet. "Are you going to call the police?" he asks, wiping his eyes with the back of a sleeve, mixing dust from the fallen masonry with his tears and the rainwater, giving his face an impressively smudged look.

"The police?" asks Le Fay, still in the terry-cloth robe Toby gave her to wear. *Where is Toby?* she wonders. *He must have run off into the night.* "Of course we're going to tell the police! A man—" She stopped. Mr. Maggs was certainly no man. "Someone *died* here tonight. We can't just ignore it and pretend it didn't happen!"

"And he was crazy and wouldn't let us go!" Albie points out.

"And . . . and . . ."

"And *no*," says Jackie. "We aren't going to tell the police. Who's going to believe a bunch of scruffy kids with a story about reanimation and not-quite-human beings . . . about brains in jars and fortune tellers . . . ? No, the matter ends here, Mulch, with the death of your master."

In amongst the smudges, a look of relief appears on Mulch's face. He even manages a smile. It's not a pretty sight.

"You've been mixed up in some bad things," says Jackie. Mulch is about to say something, but Jackie puts up her hand. She's cold and tired and wet and it's been a traumatic day . . . and they've all got to go home and face their father, who's probably worried sick about where they are and what's happened to them. "But we have a lot to thank you for too," she says.

"Woof!" agrees Fergal loudly, and trots across to Mulch and licks his fingers, those same fingers that nimbly connected his brain up to this new body. "Woof! Woof!"

"No police?" say the twins.

"No police," Jackie repeats.

"No police," Le Fay agrees, with a change of heart. "Can we take Fergal home now?"

"You'll show us a way out of here, Mulch?" Jackie asks.

"I'll do better than that. I'll drive you home," says Mulch. "You should all fit into my van."

"And then what will you do?" Le Fay asks the little man.

Mulch shrugs. He thinks of the ex-teacher of French in Lionel Lyons's old body in the apartment in town. "I'll survive," he says.

They follow him out into the rain, avoiding as many puddles as possible in the short dash to his van the color of English mustard. Le Fay sits in the front next to Mulch, with Fergal on her lap. Jackie and the twins pile into the back.

At the East Gates of Fishbone Forest, Mulch jumps out of the driver's seat, unlocks them, and drives his van out into the road. He's about to jump back out and lock the gates behind him when Le Fay puts a hand on his arm. "You don't need to do that anymore," she says, with wisdom beyond her years. "It's over, Mr. Mulch—"

"Multachan. My real name's Stefan Multachan," he corrects her. "You're right." He drives on, leaving the East Gates wide open behind them. "You're right!" It's not just common sense; somehow it's a symbolic gesture.

Mulch and the McNallys part company just around the corner from the McNallys' apartment. He stays in the van. Perhaps he's worried that they'll change their mind and inform some authority or other.

"Thank you," says Jackie from the pavement. He's not sure whether she's thanking him for the ride home or for Fergal or for what.

She's not sure either.

Le Fay steps forward, with Fergal still in her arms. They've only just been reunited and neither is in a hurry to let go.

She leans forward and speaks to Mulch in a lowered tone through the open side window of the van. Back on the curb, neither Jackie nor the twins catch what she says.

"There are no such things as bad people, Mr. Multachan," she says. "Some of us do bad things sometimes, that's all. But what you've done for us is amazing."

Fergal's approach is much more direct. He leans forward in his sister's arms and gives Mulch a great big lick across his face.

"Good-bye," mutters Mulch at last. He releases the parking brake and drives his English-mustard-colored van into the night.

The McNallys turn and head for home. It's only when they reach the doorway to their building—the single remaining door swinging on its single remaining hinge—that Jackie realizes something quite remarkable. It's stopped raining.

Whoooooooooooooosh! Forward to Tom Dwyer stepping aside to let Mulch enter the room. He looks smaller. Older. He's obviously nervous.

Fergal leaps forward and greets him, tail wagging.

Hello, Mulch! he says. *It's good to see you again. Really good! You smell fantastic!* What it comes out as is a series of woofs.

Fergal's obvious pleasure at seeing him again breaks the ice. The small man visibly relaxes a little.

"Hello, everyone," he says. "I'm glad you all came. Thank you."

Le Fay is looking past him to a bookcase. On the middle shelf is a very familiar object. It's the paperweight from Fishbone Hall, the one she slipped in the pocket of the blue robe to use as a weapon if need be. Fortunately, it hadn't been necessary.

Soon everyone is seated, and unlike the McNallys' own apartment, there are plenty of chairs for everyone . . . *and* they've all got drinks that actually taste of something. The adults are drinking orange juice (with bits in); the twins, fizzy lemonade; and Le Fay, Coke from a bottle with a straw. Le Fay has never tasted Coca-Cola before and she's never drunk anything out of a bottle with a straw. The McNallys don't have money to throw around on "non-essentials" like this, and Le Fay would be the first to admit that the whole experience is very novel. (And, whilst I remember, Tom Dwyer has given Fergal a nice big bowl of water, which he's lapping away at noisily.)

Le Fay takes the straw out of her mouth. "Why did you get Mr. Dwyer to track us down now, after all these months, Mulch?" she asks.

"Someone asked me to, Miss McNally," says Mulch. "Someone who needs your help and says that time is running out."

ChapTeR Seven

Ooooops! We're heading эmit ni ꓘɔɒd again. Lionel Lyons, who will turn out to be the last of the Lyonses of Fishbone Hall, is sitting on his father's knee. He's never sat there before. His father isn't generally a fan of using his body parts in the seating arrangements. Fortunately, Lionel is only eight years old and is good and light, and there's no danger of him wearing a patch in his father's fine trousers. His father smells of shaving soap, hair tonic, and mothballs.

"Lionel," says his father, "today I want to talk to you about duty. There is a newfangled notion that life is about enjoyment . . . about 'having a good time.' Well, not in the Lyons family, it isn't. It never has been and it never will be. Are you with me so far?"

Knowing that it's expected of him, Lionel nods his eight-year-old head wisely.

"Good chap," says his father. "You see, my boy, it is the duty of each Lyons to pass on an even bigger fortune than the one he himself has inherited on the death of his predecessor. His duty, I say. Since I inherited the Lyons millions, I have managed to make that money work for me and have turned it into more millions. It is your duty—yes, duty, little Lionel—to make sure that by the time you pass away you'll be able to leave an even bigger fortune to your son. Is that clear?"

"Yes, Father," says Lionel. Sitting on his father's knee, he has a good view out of the broken window and is watching a bird on the rotting handle of an abandoned garden shovel. He doesn't like their rare visits to the ruinous family seat of Fishbone Hall. There are very rarely any animals about—few birds, squirrels, mice, or badgers. He's pleased to see the little brown bird.

"Some families waste their money on the upkeep of huge family estates," says his father. "One of our ancestors even wasted many thousands on building this house, but later Lyons generations learned better! Yes, slave labor was used to build this house—hence the railings around the forest to discourage escape—but those slaves could have been put to work on something far more practical! Our town house is much cheaper to heat and light, which is why we live there and not here. These are things you should consider, Lionel. It all adds up." He pauses and stares into space, remembering when his own father—Lionel's grandfather Leonard Lyons—had a similar conversation with him and how it had fired his imagination and made him determined to make more and more money when his time came.

"As well as a sense of duty, Lionel," he continues, "it is vital that you as a Lyons have one other attribute. And do you know what that is?" He studies his eight-year-old son.

"Yes, Father," says Lionel.

"You do?" asks his father, somewhat surprised.

"I mean, no, Father," Lionel adds hurriedly. He was rather pleased with his wise nod and his previous "Yes, Father." He doesn't want to go and mess things up by saying the wrong thing at the wrong time now. He really *must* try to pay more attention.

The bird has hopped off the handle of the shovel and is now rooting around in the soil.

"The other attribute a Lyons needs is a thick skin," says his father. "Like a rhinoceros."

"A rhinoceros," says Lionel, who has learned from experience that repeating the last few words a grown-up has just said often makes him or her think that you have some idea what they're talking about.

"And the reason why you need such a thick skin? Because there are people out there in the big wide world who are jealous of us, Lionel. They're jealous of the way we Lyonses amassed our fortune, so they turn on us at every opportunity."

"A rhinoceros," repeats Lionel. The bird is pecking at a wriggling beetle or some such thing. *Poor beetle,* thinks little Lionel.

"What?" asks his father.

"Every opportunity," says the boy.

"Yes," agrees his father. "Absolutely. There's no shame in earning a fortune from selling weapons to both sides in foreign wars, for example, my boy. They're going to kill each other somehow anyway, and someone's got to sell them guns and ammunition. It might just as well be a Lyons. It *should* be a Lyons. It's good business sense, that's all. Who are we to judge? And piracy. Take piracy. Today piracy isn't an acceptable way to behave; of course it isn't. It's not the done thing. But back in the days when we Lyonses were pirates, some of the best families were at it . . . well, some of the more adventurous ones, at least . . . and a Lyons pirate never killed women or children. Unless they were foreign. Or it was absolutely necessary. . . ."

Lionel's father is really getting into his stride now. "And take grave robbing. There are those who see it as some barbaric act, but it wasn't as if the bodies were going to be used in some awful rituals. They were used for the advancement of science. For doctors and surgeons to get a better understanding of how the human body worked. Without graves being robbed for the dissection table, many of the surgical advances we take for granted today wouldn't exist, Lionel. It's true that we Lyonses charged good money for each body provided, but our ancestors were, yet again, providing a vital service."

The little brown bird now has a beak full of grubs and creepy-crawlies. *It must have a nest nearby,* thinks Lionel. *It must have young to feed.*

"Do you understand what I've been telling you?" asks his father.

"Yes, Papa," says Lionel. "When you die, I get all the family money and I must make even more money so that I can pass it on to my son. And it doesn't matter if other people are jealous so long as I make pots of money any way I can."

Lancaster Lyons beams with pride. He glows with pride. Every fiber of his being seems to be *humming* with pride. He gives Lionel, his only son and heir, the only hug he will ever give the boy in his entire life.

"You're a true Lyons!" he trumpets.

When I grow up, I'm not going to marry and I'm not going to have any children and I'm going to leave all of my money to lots of different charities to help people and animals and things, thinks Lionel. But he's wise enough not to speak these thoughts out loud.

"There's one thing I don't get, master," says Toby. He's wearing a T-shirt with the slogan I'M JUST THE MONKEY, ADDRESS ALL COMPLAINTS TO THE ORGAN GRINDER.

"Just the one thing?" sneers Mr. Maggs. Toby doesn't seem to get the subtle put-down. Either that or he's not bothered by it. "Well?" demands Mr. Maggs. "What is it?"

"It's just that for you to inherit all this money—"

"I assume you're referring to the Lyons family fortune."

"Yeah, that's the stuff, Mr. Maggs."

"Continue."

"Well, for you to inherit it—and for me to get my cut—Lionel Lyons Esquire needs to be dead."

Mr. Maggs stares at the boy as though he's an idiot. "He *is* dead, Toby. He died while enjoying an orange-flavored ice cream, remember? His dead body was in my fridge for I don't know how long. H—"

"Sorry, master. What I meant to say . . . what I meant was . . ." Toby is all flustered now. He doesn't like to make Mr. Maggs angry. Who in their right mind would beat a wasps' nest with a big stick? (That's a cross between a metaphor, a rhetorical question, and a very *stupid* question. In equal parts.) "What I mean is, you put that French teacher brain your Cousin Ralphie sent you into Lionel Lyons's body so that he could *appear* to be alive—"

"Yes," agrees Mr. Maggs. "Guilty as charged! The shame! The shame!" He suppresses a giggle. "And we toddled off together to the poky little offices of the over-stuffed Mr. Fudge of Garland & Fudge and my pretend Lionel Lyons wrote a nice big official will leaving everything to *me* when he dies!"

Mr. Maggs puts his hands above his head and does a triumphant little pirouette like a ballerina . . . at least it would be like a ballerina if ballerinas had pumpkin-shaped heads and rows of pointy little teeth. He comes to a halt. "Oh, I see what you mean, my spiky-haired boy! You're thinking that I'm going to have to take away the patient's life in order to claim my fortune!"

"Yes, master. That's it."

"And Toby-Woby isn't happy with the idea?" He sticks out his lower lip and pouts.

"Well, the truth be told, Mr. Maggs, not really."

"But you knew what this project would involve when I hired you. You knew that the ultimate goal was implementing my *Manifesto of Change* and that for this I'll need the Lyons fortune, and for that—"

"Yes, but I hadn't thought that far ahead," Toby protests. "I hadn't thought of all the little details."

"What's that saying, Toby? Ah, yes. The *devil* is in the details . . . and if you think killing a man is a small detail . . ."

"I didn't say that," Toby protests. "Well, that's not what I meant anyway."

Mr. Maggs comes in close. "Want to know a secret? Promise not to tell? *We aren't going to harm a hair on the patient's head.*"

Toby visibly relaxes. It's like there's a great weight off his mind. "We're not?"

"No, we're just going to make him *think* that we are."

"But I don't understand, master. What good will that do?"

"Simple. Now that he's tricked ancient old Fudge of Garland & Fudge, he's fulfilled his purpose. His work is done and dusted. I don't need his dead body to get a death certificate. I've got death certificates coming out of my ears."

Toby finds himself looking at Mr. Maggs's ears to see if he means it literally. The master doesn't usually use such colorful language. What he doesn't know is that Mr. Maggs spent much of last night reading a book of colloquialisms—everyday phrases—to improve his language skills to help him to blend in when he finally implements his *Manifesto of Change* and ventures out into the big wild world again.

"So what happens to the French teacher?" says Toby.

"Well, we can't have him walking around as Lionel Lyons once I've told old Fudge that he's dead."

"Yeah, that could really mess things up," agrees Toby.

"And we can't have him telling everyone that he's really Mr. Thomas Dwyer either, now, can we?"

"No."

"So what we need to do is make sure that he goes into hiding. Lies low. Keeps his trap shut."

"Uh-huh." Toby nods. "But what if he doesn't agree to?"

"This is where my enormous brain comes in!" grins Mr. Maggs.

Which is why you have such an enormous head! Toby thinks but, like young Lionel Lyons on his father's knee all those years before, very wisely doesn't say what he's thinking out loud. "What have you come up with?" he says instead.

"We let Monsieur Dwyer *think* that we're going to have to kill him and make him go into hiding."

"In other words, making him think that going into hiding is his own choice. That's BRILLIANT, Mr. Maggs!"

"Some of us are born great, Toby," beams his master. "I'll get Mulch to sneak him out one evening. Little does Dwyer know that it's with my seal of approval!" With that, Mr. Maggs throws himself into his chair behind his desk. It's sodden with rainwater from a leak in the ceiling—well, a hole open to the sky, actually—directly above it. He leans back and picks up Duffel from the floor. "Why didn't the mother horse hear her tiny foal's cry?"

For a fleeting moment, Toby is thrown by the sudden switch of subject. Then he realizes that it's one of Mr. Maggs's riddles.

"I don't know, Mr. Maggs. Why didn't the mother horse hear her tiny foal's cry?"

"Because it was a little horse. A little horse. A little hoarse: *h-o-a-r-s-e*. Do you understand?"

"Yes . . . yes, of course. Very good, master. I must go and get lunch ready."

"Very well," says Mr. Maggs. "Soup would be nice. A pink soup. Yes, let's have pink soup." He gives Duffel an extra hug. Of course, the teddy bear remains absolutely silent, as teddy bears do.

"Until this week, the only person I've seen from the master's house"—he means Fishbone Hall, of course—"is Tom," says Mulch. He looks across at Dwyer, who is sipping his orange juice. "We've been sharing this apartment since the day Mr. Maggs died. Since that day, I haven't seen Toby and I hadn't—"

"Seen us—"

"—until now," the twins interrupt.

"It wasn't you I was—er—referring to," says Mulch.

"Who, then?" asks Jackie.

"A few days ago I made contact with Duffel," says Mulch, as though it would mean something to the assembled company.

The McNallys look at each other blankly, as if to say: *Are we supposed to know who Duffel is?*

"Who?" asks Le Fay.

"Sorry," says Mulch. "Of course you don't know him by name. Mr. Maggs's teddy bear, Duffel."

Albie laughs. "You found his teddy?"

"That's nice," says Josh.

"But he was clutching it when he fell into that hole," says Jackie. He was even singing about the pair of them on the way down, she remembers with a shudder. "You didn't climb down into the hole, did you?" she asks. Had he crawled all the way down into the darkness to try to rescue Mr. Maggs or to bring up what was left of him?

"No," says Mulch with a shake of the head. "You see, the thing is . . ." He pauses for a moment and runs a finger around the rim of his glass. It makes a whining sound—and no jokes about "whine glasses," please. "You see . . . it was Duffel who crawled *out*."

Jackie gives him the benefit of one of her funny looks. Not funny ha ha but funny peculiar. It's the kind of look that says, *Pull the other one, matey, it's got bells on.*

"The teddy bear crawled out?" says Le Fay.

"And tracked me down," says Mulch. "All the way up here to this apartment."

"And this teddy bear—"

"Duffel."

"And Duffel walked into the foyer downstairs, past a security guard who can detect a dog scuttling across the floor without even having to look out from behind his newspaper, and came up the stairs or in the elevator—"

"The stairs, I suspect," says Mulch. "I don't think he's tall enough to press the elevator button to this floor."

"—or in the elevator," Le Fay continues, "and knocked on your front door."

"Because he couldn't reach the bell." Mulch nods.

"And nobody thought it was strange that there was a teddy bear taking a stroll around the place?"

"Le Fay!" snaps Jackie. She's brought the others up to be polite, and crazy though Mulch's claims are, there's no need for her sister to sound so . . . so sarcastic.

"Sorry," says Le Fay, sucking another slurp of Coke through her bendy straw. "But you must admit that it sounds a little odd."

"And unless you're in the know, so does the idea of walking around in someone else's body," Dwyer points out.

"Woof!" Fergal agrees.

"Or turning into a jackal," says a voice from the doorway.

Five pairs of McNally eyes turn to the doorway. In it stands a rather battered, threadbare-looking teddy . . .

. . . which would be quite a dramatic entrance, I suppose, if he didn't look quite so *saggy*.

ChapTeR EighT

"We've already met," says Duffel, his arms flopping teddy bear–like to his sides, which is hardly surprising. He walks rather awkwardly into the center of the room. "Don't look so shocked by a walking, talking teddy bear," he says. "You of all people have no reason to! Tom Dwyer and you"—he lifts a paw and points to Fergal—"are out and about thanks to borrowed bodies and you"—he looks Jackie straight in the eye—"have some remarkable transmogrifying abilities of your own."

"Is that a word?" asks Josh.

"If it isn't it should be," says Albie.

"Shhh!" says Le Fay.

"How did you know?" demands Jackie, assuming that *transmogrifying* must be another term for shape shifting or turning-into-a-jackal-and-then-back-again.

"I've been watching you," admits Duffel. "All of you."

"*Why?*" ask Jackie, Le Fay, and the twins.

"Woof?" asks Fergal.

Duffel heaves himself up onto the sofa between Mulch and Tom Dwyer. Le Fay notices Mulch edge away from him, perhaps to give the new arrival more room or perhaps because he feels uneasy in his company.

"I need help," says Duffel. "It's a unique and delicate matter, and I think that anyone who's faced up to Mr. Maggs and has a brother who's now, on the outside at least, a—er—*dog* would have a better understanding of things than most. . . ."

"So you decided to check us out?" asks Le Fay, the half-drunk bottle of Coke now completely ignored on a side table.

"Yes," says Duffel.

I'm having a conversation with a teddy bear, thinks Le Fay.

"How did you find us?" asks Josh.

"I think we'd have noticed a bear following us," adds Albie. "Even if he was wearing a hat and a raincoat with a turned-up collar."

"I found Mulch. That was easy. I knew about this apartment here in town—"

"And he already knew where *we* live because he drove us home the night . . ." Jackie falters.

"The night that me and Mr. Maggs were swallowed up in that rip. Yes."

"That what?" ask the twins.

"That hole," says Duffel.

"If you don't mind me asking, how come you weren't killed?" asks Jackie. "That was a very deep hole and it opened up very suddenly."

"Isn't the question how come you were alive in the first place?" asks Le Fay. "I thought most teddies were filled with stuffing. Don't tell me Mr. Maggs somehow managed to put a brain in you too?"

Duffel shakes his badly stitched head. "No. Mine is a very different story. As to how I didn't die . . . I not only have plenty of padding—"

"But you also landed on Mr. Maggs," says Le Fay.

"Yes," says Duffel, his voice barely above a whisper.

Jackie is still far from happy that someone—more than some*one*—outside her family and very close circle of friends knows her secret. Now it seems that this extraordinary ragbag of a trio, comprising a petty crook who stole brains to order, a French teacher in an old man's body, and a teddy bear, all know about it too! How safe a secret is that?!?

"What's this delicate matter you think we can help you with, Duffel?" asks Le Fay.

"I need to put a stop to the rips—the outbreak of holes."

"And because of what we've seen and what we've been through, you think me and a bunch of scrawny kids—"

Fergal barks.

"—and Fergal can help you?" says Jackie.

"Teddy bears can't be too picky when it comes to seeking assistance," says Duffel. "And don't undersell yourselves."

"We certainly have looks," says Albie.

"And charm," says Josh.

"And intelligence," says Duffel, his eyes once again on Le Fay.

"Do you know something about me I don't?" she demands.

"I'm simply wondering whether a family with a sister who can turn into a jackal might also have siblings with other talents," says Duffel. This time he stares at the twins, remembering the strange incident he'd witnessed at Garland Park when one of them—he can't tell which—had that amazing ballooning arm!

"My abilities have been a secret up until now. . . . At least, I thought they were," says Jackie. "I'd very much like to keep it that way."

"Who are we going to tell?" says Tom Dwyer. "We three are the biggest bunch of misfits I've ever been a part of." It's the first time the McNallys have seen him smile.

"It's difficult for a talking teddy bear to get taken seriously. Lionel Lyons is supposed to be dead, and Mulch here is . . . Mulch," Duffel shrugs. A shrugging teddy bear is a strange sight to behold.

"In all the time I worked for the master," says Mulch, "I never knew Duffel was alive. I simply assumed that he was a well-loved stuffed toy. I still find it hard to believe. . . ." He looks hurt, upset that Mr. Maggs had kept such an important truth from him. "I was at a loss for words when he first arrived at our door."

"So our secret's safe with you?" asks Jackie. "If we don't have your word on that—from all three of you—we're not even going to stay here and listen to a thing you say, let alone even think of helping you."

"Though we *are* going to finish our drinks first," says Albie.

"Absolutely," says Josh, gulping at his glass of lemonade.

"No one's going to tell anyone anything," says Duffel. "We promise you that."

"I promise," says Tom.

"Me too," says Mulch.

"We all have plenty to hide," says Duffel.

"Which brings us back to you wanting our help," says Le Fay. "What is it that you'd like us to do?"

"Three things. I'd like you to trust me. I'd like you to come with me now, and I'd like you to help me to try to stop this outbreak of holes. In return, I offer you a glimmer of hope. A possibility—and only that—a possibility that we might be able to bring Fergal back to how he was."

Fergal's ears prick up. He raises his doggy head, his doggy tongue still lolling from the side of his doggy mouth.

"But that's impossible!" gasps Mulch. "You never said anything about—"

"There's plenty I haven't told you, Mulch," Duffel confesses, putting a paw on the little man's hand. Mulch jerks it away as though he's received an electric shock. "I'm sorry." Duffel looks directly at Le Fay. "But I won't lie to you. Will you come with me now?" For some reason four pairs of McNally eyes turn to Le Fay to see what she wants to do.

There's something that anthropologists or psychologists (or some such -ologists) call "the group dynamic." The group dynamic is the way a bunch of people or animals behave *as* a group as a result of the way roles are formed and individuals behave *within* that group. In groups of animals, it's often the Alpha Male—the biggest, strongest, wisest male animal—who is in charge. As he gets older, he's challenged by younger males, and in the end, one of these becomes the new Alpha Male and the new boss of the group. Then the group dynamic changes, because he has different favorites amongst the other members of the group and different ideas as to where they should go next to feed or what they should do.

The group dynamic in the McNally household used to mean that poor old oldest sister Jackie did just about everything whilst their dad, Captain Rufus McNally (retired), sat in the back room emptying bottles. If any decisions needed to be made for the welfare of her siblings, Le Fay, Albie and Josh, and Fergal, it was Jackie who made them. They relied on her and looked up to her. Sometimes they grumbled that she "wasn't fair," but in their heart of hearts they knew that she was trying to do what was best for them. Add to this the fact that she could turn into a jackal, and she made a very good leader!

Now, following Le Fay's winning a place in the Tap 'n' Type finals and Fergal's dreadful fall, the group dynamic has subtly begun to change, so subtly to begin with that none of them has really noticed, including Le Fay herself. More and more, she is now the one with the knowledge, the ideas, and the gut feelings. The McNallys are acting more and more on her suggestions and advice.

It's obvious to everyone in the room that, rightly or wrongly, everything now rests on her decision whether to go with Duffel or not.

"We'll come," says Le Fay.

The hands on the clock go backward. The dates on the calendar run in reverse. Here we go again:

Smeek and Doyle bury what's left of Byron—mainly her bloodstained jumpsuit with **BYRON** on the breast pocket—in the sand, which is much cooler the farther down they dig with their hands. This is partly out of respect for their fellow escapee and partly to try to cover their tracks should anyone discover their coordinates and come through the Doughnut in search of them. Smeek has torn off strips of his clothing to bandage Carbonet. Add to that the fact that great clumps of his hair are falling out—a side effect of coming through the Doughnut that doesn't seem to have affected the others (the hair in Carbonet's ears, for example, being one of the few things about him that doesn't appear to have been horribly mutilated by his recent experience) and the (very) strange numbers of toes on Smeek's feet—and you'll appreciate what a strange sight he is . . . not that anyone is likely to *see* any of them out here in the desert in the dark.

"Time to move, old friend," Smeek tells Carbonet, another hank of hair falling from his head.

"You're going to have to pull it all out before we go anywhere," says Doyle.

"What?"

"Your hair, Smeek."

"Why?"

"Because if we're going to be carrying Carbonet, we can't keep stopping every few feet to put him down and pick it up!"

"But I don't need to keep it!"

"You're missing the point, genius," says Doyle. "Your clumps of hair will leave a trail . . . a trail that anyone can follow in daylight."

"But we'll be leaving footprints anyway!" Smeek protests.

But Doyle isn't going to argue. He grabs the end of as much of Smeek's remaining long black locks as possible . . . and the hair comes away from Smeek's head surprisingly easily and painlessly. "There," says Doyle. He hands it to a very bald-looking Smeek, whose head now resembles nothing more than a pumpkin with a shark's-teeth smile. "Now shall we get going?"

"A br-broom," rasps Carbonet. "I can use . . . your h-h-air . . . as a broom." Every word is a terrible effort. Blood trickles from the corner of his mouth.

Smeek manages to force a smile. "Good idea, friend," he says. "But do lie still."

Doyle wonders if Carbonet is delirious but soon sees what the wounded man means. As he and Smeek carry

Carbonet between them, Carbonet just manages to keep a hold on the long tress of Smeek's hair between his remaining bloodied fingers, letting it trail on the ground behind them, brushing the sand so as to obscure, if not completely erase, their footprints. Using this method, just a light breeze blowing the surface of the desert could virtually obliterate their trail altogether.

They have been walking for a few hours when the trio have their first piece of luck: Doyle spots a shack—well, he almost walks smack into it. This is soon followed by their second: inside the shack, they find a hurricane lamp for light and a few basics, including bottled water.

Carefully lying Carbonet on a table, Smeek opens a bottle and holds it to his injured friend's lips. "Drink," he says.

Not far from Tom Dwyer and Mulch's apartment is an old bakery. It's disused now since the owner, Donald Lumpit of Lumpit's Loaves, died without a will and a dispute arose between ten of his eleven children. (The eleventh child—the third-oldest girl, Iris—is a marine biologist shipwrecked on an island paradise somewhere and doesn't even know that her dad has passed away.) As the legal wrangle continues as to who owns what and who should be in charge of which department, the baker's production has ground to a halt, without a single Lumpit's loaf bouncing off the end of the conveyor belt in over two years, and the building and the machinery it houses are falling into disrepair. It is here that Duffel has asked the McNallys to bring him.

"It's easier if you carry me," he tells Le Fay, "and I'll whisper directions."

On the way, Albie and Josh do plenty of burping and belching. (I use both words in case there's a difference. The word *belch* somehow suggests something deeper and wetter to me.) The twins aren't used to drinking carbonated drinks, and the fizzy lemonade they had at the Garland Apartment Building is taking its toll. Up front, Le Fay carries Duffel (who's heavy but not *that* heavy), with Jackie and Fergal at the rear. This weather really is far too hot for dogs, and Fergal is panting badly.

When they finally reach the boarded-up building, Duffel has Le Fay put him down in an alleyway running up the side of the bakery, and whilst the twins stand at the end of the alley to check that there's no one coming—Fergal seated between them on the hot pavement, thinking back to the days before thick fur—Duffel shows them his secret way in through a basement window.

Fergal leaps in last of all and is delighted by the coolness of the shade.

Duffel has made a small area of living space for himself in the middle of a vast room, having gathered together pieces of furniture from various parts of the old bakery.

Once the McNallys are settled, he begins to talk. "What I'm about to tell you will sound completely crazy," says Duffel, "but as I've said before, if anyone's going to believe me, you will."

"Go on," says Jackie.

"Let me start with the easy part," says the teddy bear. "Do you know what a time-share is?"

No prizes for guessing that it's Le Fay who answers. "It's a place—like a vacation home, for example—owned by a whole bunch of people who get to live in it at different times of year," she says.

"How does that work, then?" asks Josh, absentmindedly scratching Fergal between his doggy ears just the way he likes it and just the way Mr. Maggs had sometimes scratched Duffel.

Le Fay switches into brainy sister mode. "Well, say six people buy equal shares in a time-share; that would mean they each get to stay in the house for two months of every year," she explains.

"Huh?" asks Albie, if "Huh?" counts as a question.

"Twelve months divided by six people equals two months each," Jackie points out.

"Simple!" Albie laughs.

"It's a way of sort of owning a place you could never afford on your own and having it to yourself, but only for set times of the year," says Le Fay. "When you're there, it's all yours and yours alone. That's right, isn't it, Duffel?"

Duffel nods his badly stitched head.

"You sure know a lot of stuff, sis," Albie says to Le Fay, clearly impressed. "But what do time-shares have to do—"

"—with stopping the outbreak of holes?" asks Jackie. "You didn't bring us here to go into the vacation homes business."

Josh looks a little put out. It's *his* job to finish his twin's sentences for him and vice versa.

"There are lots of different ways of time-sharing," Duffel explains, pacing up and down in front of a giant dough-mixing machine, which looks like it mixed its last dough a long, long time ago. "You can time-share a bed, for example."

"A bed?" say Albie and Josh.

"He's right, you know," says Jackie, remembering something their father, Captain Rufus, once told her. "Dad's brother, Uncle Erik, used to share a bed. He did dishes in a restaurant kitchen during the day and slept in the bed at night, and someone else, who did dishes in the restaurant kitchen during the night, slept in the same bed during the day. They hardly ever even saw each other!"

"Okay," says Duffel, still pacing. "That's the easy part. Think of time-sharing. . . . Now it gets—er—more complicated. As you probably know, the world's population is getting bigger and bigger all the time. People call it the population explosion. There's only a finite—only a certain amount—of land on this planet that people can live on, and there are more and more people needing to share it." He stops.

"Woof!" says Fergal. What he's trying to say is *Go on!*

"In the future, the problem will get so serious that people will try to come up with all sorts of different solutions: space solutions, colonizing the moon, floating cities . . . the kind of things you see in science-fiction movies and television programs." Duffel doesn't realize that the McNallys have never owned a TV set.

"I still don't see—"

Duffel stops walking and turns to face them all. "Someone once said—or will one day say, I can't remember which—that the past is just another country or some such thing. If you think of it in that way, then the past could be used as another country *for people to colonize.* A way of helping to solve the population explosion would be to send people back in time to live in the past, where there are fewer people and there's more room."

"But that's crazy!" says Jackie.

"It's ingenious," Duffel argues. "You can have a huge number of people all born in the present, living on the same small plot of land but in different times in the past when it was previously unoccupied!"

ChaPTeR Nine

Albie giggles. He can't help it. "Are you trying to tell us that people have been trying to travel back in time to time-share this planet in the past?"

"Not exactly," says Duffel. "What I'm trying to tell you is that people from the future have tried to travel back into their past and have succeeded."

Le Fay stares into Duffel's glassy eyes. "And the future's past is our present, *here and now*," she adds, her head buzzing with all the implications.

Duffel nods again. "Yes."

"But surely we'd notice if people suddenly started appearing out of nowhere—?" begins Albie.

"And what if people start running into their grown-up great-grandchildren who haven't even been born yet?" says Josh.

"And tried sleeping in our beds and stuff?" asks Albie.

"I think we might notice them if they did!" says Josh.

"Who's been sleeping in my bed?" says Albie, putting on a deep gruff voice.

"Said Papa Bear," says Josh. Then, remembering who he's talking to, becomes suitably embarrassed and falls silent.

Duffel seizes this embarrassment as an opportunity to continue. "Scientists from the future spent years trying to develop time travel but got nowhere," he explains. "The best minds in the world were working on it, but they just couldn't find a way. Then one day, out of the blue, the authorities stumbled on someone who had built his own time machine using completely alien technology—"

"And was that someone an alien himself, by any chance?" Le Fay blurts out, barely able to contain her growing excitement as the pieces of the jigsaw fall into place.

"Kind of," says Duffel.

"And was . . . is . . . will his name be Mr. Maggs?" cries Le Fay.

"Yes," says Duffel, "though in the future, his name is Smeek. It's only in your time that he took the name Maggs."

"Mr. Maggs was an alien—" gasps Albie.

"—from the future!" gasps Josh.

"And you're from the future too," states Jackie, who's been listening silently from the sidelines.

"Yes," says Duffel.

"WOW!" say the twins.

There is a brief silence. "Tell us what happened. . . . I mean, what *will* happen," says Le Fay.

Duffel wipes his threadbare forehead with a paw. He has their undivided attention. "In the future, space—not the twinkling-stars-in-the-sky kind but the room-to-move variety—is at a premium. Most people live in small high-rise apartments—skyscrapers—because they take up the least room. In one particular skyscraper the local police were getting more and more complaints from residents that the new tenant, a long-haired guy called Smeek, was—"

"Long-haired!" Albie cries out in amazement.

"Shhh!" says Jackie.

"—that Smeek was making a lot of noise in his apartment day and night, and whatever it was that he was up to, he was causing the walls to shake. After a number of warnings, the police gained entry to the apartment and found an extraordinary homemade machine in his bathroom. Smeek was taken away for questioning, because he didn't have the papers required to be a resident there . . . and even more importantly, because he didn't look quite *normal!*"

"Woof!" Fergal urges. *Go on!*

"During the course of his questioning, Smeek claimed not to be human, and there were those who were quick to brand him a liar or a madman. Only his machine—which was like a metal ring, big enough for a single man to crawl through—led to his being taken seriously. A few simple tests with animals proved that he had built a machine that could send living creatures through time. A rabbit was sent into the following Tuesday, and I seem

to remember something about a gerbil and a previous Saturday."

"W—!" says Albie.

"—ow!" says Josh.

"The potential for using Mr. Maggs's—Smeek's— equipment to help solve the population problem was spotted immediately. The problem was Smeek himself. The authorities didn't want an alien to have anything to do with the project. They knew that they'd have to choose the time and place to send people to with incred- ible care. Mess about with Time without rules and who knew what might happen? So they locked him up. Don't go thinking that society will be any more tolerant in the future."

"I'm finding this very hard to believe, Duffel," says Jackie.

"Here we are listening to a teddy bear, and you're telling me what he says sounds unbelievable?" says Josh. "Our life is unbelievable!"

"It's just one unlikely exploit after another," adds Le Fay in agreement. (It's this comment that gave me the idea for the title of this series.) "And the holes?"

"I'm coming to them," says Duffel. "Smeek was locked away with some other prisoners considered high-security risks while top-secret experiments were carried out on his Doughnut."

"His *what?*" asks an incredulous Albie.

"His machine," Duffel explains. "The scientists named it Doughnut I because of its appearance. They built a bigger version—Doughnut II—based on the original specifications and kept it in a wing of the prison where Smeek was being kept so that they could haul him out of his cell and get him to explain things if they needed to."

Le Fay thinks back to the Smeek she knew: the Mr. Maggs who loved riddles and his teddy bear and whose *Manifesto of Change* contained simple and childish ideals. She felt bad that humans had treated him—sorry, that should be *would one day* treat him—this way.

"So did the experiments work?" asks Jackie. "Are we now time-sharing our present with people from the future?"

Duffel sits down on an upturned plastic crate labeled TUMPIT'S TOVAES. "Not when I left. You see, Smeek and a few other prisoners managed to escape from the cell they were sharing and to get to the Doughnut and jump through it into this time frame, but something went wrong. . . ."

Inside the shack.

"I'm going to have to operate," says Smeek.

"What, are you crazy?" says Doyle, looking around the shack. "This place is filthy, we don't have any anesthetic, you don't have any tools—"

Smeek pulls open a drawer in the table. There are three sharp wooden-handled knives. "I have no choice, Doyle!" he says. "Carbonet's going to die if I don't do anything. We need to find a way of boiling some of the water and we need something to use as thread for stitching. . . . HELP ME!"

"Keep your hair on!" says Doyle, and then, seeing how completely bald his once-hairy cellmate now is, he laughs. "Your hair!" he says. "We could twist the strands to make thread. Now, what about a needle?"

They frantically search the shack, trying to find anything and everything that might possibly play a part—however tiny—in increasing the chances of saving Carbonet's life.

Smeek finds the old teddy bear under an upturned tin bathtub in a corner. He holds it up triumphantly. "Just what we need to help him keep his body shape!" he announces.

The operation takes fourteen hours. Doyle spends some of the time assisting Smeek, some of it being sick outside, some of it trying to sleep and to keep warm as the nighttime temperatures drop even farther, and some of it trying to keep cool. The details of the surgery itself are gory and Smeek's skills under such near-impossible conditions are incredible. At first working by light from the old hurricane lamp (also used to heat the knives and

boil the water), now hanging from a crossbeam, and later from the glaring sun, filtered through a burlap-sack curtain covering the one window, he cuts, stitches, cauterizes, sets, and generally repairs Carbonet's internal organs, skin, and bones, somehow holding the man together inside a padded suit made from the teddy bear, making the man and the material one.

"Mr. Maggs saved your life," says Le Fay when Duffel has finished telling them of this extraordinary operation.

"He did," he says quietly, turning away, but Fergal clearly sees the tears seeping out from beneath Duffel's glass eyes. "Once I'd recovered enough and we reached civilization, he did further operations to make me as you see me today. . . . I was horribly mutilated when I came through the Doughnut and something went wrong. Now I don't know where the teddy bear ends and I begin. It's unlikely anyone else could have done what Mr. Maggs, as you know him, did. He was a remarkable scientist and surgeon and a true friend." Le Fay goes over to Duffel and gives him a hug. Somehow it seems an okay thing to do to a teddy bear without asking.

"What did you do?" asks Jackie. Her words sound harsh.

"Do?" Duffel sniffs.

"What did you do—*will* you do or whatever—to end up sharing a cell with Mr. Maggs as a high-risk prisoner? What was your crime?"

"That's the awful thing," says Duffel, somehow managing to look more forlorn than any of the McNallys have seen him in the brief time they've know him. "I was a government plant. . . . I was working undercover, pretending to be a prisoner in order to befriend Smeek and to find out as much about him as possible."

"Then why didn't you stop him from jumping through the Doughnut?"

"Because by then I was on his side. I *wanted* him to escape. After months of spending time together before the escape, I came to believe that what we were doing to him was wrong . . . especially when I realized what kind of alien he really was."

"What planet was he from?" asks an excited twin. (It's hard to tell which one. They both look so similar.)

"Earth," says Duffel.

"You mean—?"

"Yes," says Duffel. "He was not only from your future but from my future too . . . from ahead of *my* time. The Mr. Maggs you met was not human in the sense that he wasn't standard *Homo sapiens sapiens* like you or I. He was a member of the next stage of evolution. He is what we will become."

At exactly the same moment that Duffel is making this startling revelation, Count Medoc Silverman is driving his Bentley into the garage next to the stable block of his home, and the garage door is automatically closing slowly behind him. To any casual observer, the chairman and owner of Tap 'n' Type looks as smooth and unruffled as always. But inside? Inside he's a very worried man.

Since Duffel came to see him—or Carbonet, as he'll always think of him, however dreadful a freak he's become since Smeek put him back together—Medoc has been afraid.

Duffel had talked wildly and passionately about how important it is that they go back to their own time. About how their presence here is causing "rips"—the outbreak of holes—because they've somehow messed with the Space-Time Continuum. But what does he know?

Medoc had wanted to know how their going back might help to put things right. Duffel's answer had been unimpressively vague: "It's not so much putting things right as stopping making things worse," he'd said. "Every little thing we do in this time is changing history. It's wrong. If we can get back to our own time, at least we won't be making things even more *wrong*."

Medoc walks out of the side door of the garage and toward the house. Go back? The little freak must be joking. Back in his own time, Count Medoc Silverman was nothing more than a man in a slate gray jumpsuit with **DOYLE** printed above his breast pocket and had nothing to look forward to except an endless prison sentence for a series of frauds involving missing government gold— boy, does he love gold—and computers.

Here, on the other hand, he is a success. A free man. He isn't harming anyone. Okay, so that isn't strictly true.

If he hadn't been here in this time, there would never have been a Tap 'n' Type company, so there would never have been a Tap 'n' Type–sponsored competition, so that poor kid would never have fallen out of the window . . . but start making tenuous connections like that and everyone in the world will find themselves responsible in some way, shape, or form for some accident or other. No! Medoc is staying put. . . .

Wait a minute. That's not strictly true either.

Medoc lets himself in through his front door with a gold key, switches off the internal alarm system, and makes his way straight to his vast workshop, which he also has to unlock before entering. Much of the room is taken up with his own version of the Doughnut, put together over the years from the blueprints he stole that day they escaped from their cell and jumped through Doughnut II. He found the plans—the schematics showing every single component of the time machine and how to assemble them—in a drawer when he and the other three were heaving furniture around to build that barricade against the door. He slipped them inside his jumpsuit without the others ever noticing . . . and now here are the results of his labor.

Some of the pieces were easy to lay hands on. Some he bought in hardware stores; some he ordered through his factory; some he had specially made. Money can buy you anything. He smiles to himself. There's Carbonet (or Duffel, or whatever he chooses to call himself these days) thinking that these rips—these holes—are caused by their mere presence in this time. Little does he realize that they're a side effect of using his very own Dough-nut . . . which is why the holes are restricted to this particular country at this particular time. He's just glad that his tests haven't caused the really big flash-bang-wallop that occurred the first time they used Doughnut II in a real hurry. That would be most unfortunate. But the holes have only swallowed up a few miles of earth here and there. The odd building and motor vehicle. That's a small price to pay. . . .

The count presses a button and his workshop is suddenly flooded with the sound of jazz, playing from hidden speakers dotted about the room. He starts humming along to the hip-hap-happy tune. Life is *gooooooood*, and there's work to be done.

ChapTer Ten

"So you want us to help you to convince this man Doyle to somehow go back with you to your own time?" says Le Fay once Duffel has finished explaining his plans.

"Er, yes."

"And by saying 'convince,' what you really mean is *force him to* if necessary?"

"Er, yes."

"And how do you propose to do that?"

"Er, well, there are six of us and only one of him . . . and two of you can appear to be vicious dogs—well, a dog and a jackal—if need be."

"You talk in a very old-fashioned way for someone from the future," says Albie.

"Yeah," says Josh. "Aren't there a whole load of new words and phrases we've never heard of—"

"—and what do people wear? Silver suits and—"

"You could be putting us in danger," says Jackie.

"Er, yes," agrees Duffel, "but I really think you're my only hope. And if we *don't* do anything, these rips—this outbreak of holes—could end up doing some very serious damage indeed."

Le Fay, who has been sitting in silence at the sidelines, stands up. "You haven't said *how* you intend to get you and Doyle back to your time."

"Doyle has somehow managed to build himself a Doughnut, but he doesn't know that I know that."

"You have been a busy bear," says Le Fay. "Jackie, why don't—"

She's interrupted by Albie, but not by one of his quick quips or jokey jokes. He groans and falls forward off an old office chair. As he hits the cold bakery floor, he starts to grow—not just his arm but all of him. His clothes, everything. He's getting bigger and bigger all over before their very eyes. As he grows, his body lets off a strange rumbling sound, like the worst collywobbles anyone's tummy has ever had. In less than fifteen seconds the rumbling has stopped and so has Albie's growing. He gets to his (extra-large) knees, then to his (extra-large) feet, and stands up. He's over twenty feet tall. If this was an ordinary room, not a vast empty bakery, there's no way he'd be able to stand to his full height.

Everyone is flabbergasted. Fergal does a frightened-doggy widdle—there's a Bumbo side to him, remember—Duffel sits down with a bump that must hurt him, padding or no padding, and Jackie and Le Fay gawk, but it is Josh who is most stunned. All of his life, he and his twin have looked almost identical. It's been near impossible to tell them apart. And now there's no doubt who's who. Albie is the twenty-foot-tall one. Josh finds himself crying.

Albie leans forward to take his twin's hand. "IT'S OKAY, JOSH," he says. "I'M OKAY." He's startled by the loud booming of his own voice. He wasn't planning on speaking louder, but with his huge chest and lungs, that's just the way it came out. Josh's hand looks tiny in his.

Five, four, three, two, one. Jump! We're back in time again (depending on one's starting point, of course). As Melvyn Gottlieb will so neatly put it (one day): "When you're dealing in time travel, the terms *backward* and *forward* are little more than matters of opinion."

We're in a room. It's very small and very neat and tidy. There's a woman in the room, sitting by a window, looking out to the street below. In one arm she holds a baby boy. In the other she holds another boy, the same age and almost identical to the other. She is talking to the one on her right.

"And now I must name you, little one," she says with that unique love in her voice that only a mother can have for her child. "And your name will be the only clue to the power that I can see you'll one day hold."

There's a squeak as a doorknob turns, followed by a creak as the door opens. In steps the dashing, uniformed figure of a young sea captain.

"Rufus!" beams the woman.

"Hello, Freya," says the man, bending forward and kissing his wife on the forehead. If love were light, this room would be flooded in brilliant sunshine. "The twins not asleep yet?"

"Today's the day I'm naming them," Freya McNally explains. "This is Joshua," she says.

"Hello, Joshua," says Captain Rufus, tickling his son under the chin. Joshua is kind enough to give him a smile in return. "And what name have you given this other fine chap?" he asks, turning to the other.

"I was about to tell this little one that his name is Albion," she says.

"Josh and Albie," smiles Rufus.

"Albion and Joshua," smiles Freya.

"Can I go and tell Jackie and Le Fay their brothers' names?" asks Captain McNally excitedly.

"Of course," says Freya.

It is only when her husband has left the room that she turns back to Albie. "I have named you after Albion, son of Neptune. Giant among men," she says. But of course, he is far too young to understand a word his mum is saying.

"Googa," gurgles Albie.

"Gaga," gurgles Josh.

"WHAT DO I DO, JACKS?" pleads Albie, his voice echoing around the abandoned bakery.

"Try whispering, for a start," says Jackie, trying to calm him down. "There's no need to panic."

"SORRY," says Albie, lowering his tone. "HOW DO I GET BACK TO MY NORMAL SIZE?"

"How should she know?" says Josh, still staring up at his enormous twin in disbelief.

"HOW DO YOU GET BACK TO BEING A HUMAN SHAPE WHEN YOU'RE A JACKAL?"

"I've told you loads of times," says Jackie. "I just think it."

"SO I SHOULD THINK MYSELF BACK INTO BEING SMALL?" asks Albie.

"Give it a try," says Jackie. "Once you've got the hang of it, I'm sure you'll find it easier and easier."

Albie frowns a giant frown across his giant forehead and really concentrates.

Fergal jumps up in front of him, barking. What he's trying to say is: *You may look different, but you still smell just the same!*

"IT'S NOT WOR-king!" Albie cries, but by the time he's finished saying it he's back to being exactly the same size as Josh, and the twins give each other a big hug.

"Now think big," says Le Fay.

"What?" asks Albie.

"See if you can think yourself into your giant form," says Le Fay.

"Okay," says Albie, and seconds later he's growing again.

Now that he's got the hang of it, he GROWS and shrinks back to normal, GROWS and shrinks back to normal, GROWS—

"That's enough!" laughs Le Fay. "We've got to get going!"

"I knew that you McNallys were right for this task!" says Duffel. "That newfound talent of yours could come in very handy."

All fears of Albie's sudden discovery and transformation are forgotten and are replaced with a feeling of excitement and possibility.

"You know what this means, don't you?" Albie says to Josh.

"What?"

"That your secret power will probably be revealed soon. I mean, we're the same age and everything. It's more than likely."

"I suppose," says Josh, "but I'll probably turn out to be able to shrink to the size of a mouse, and one of you will tread on me by mistake." He doesn't want to be jealous. He really doesn't. It's just that not only has his brother beaten him to finding out his secret power, but it's also a really *cool* one. He can't hope to compete with that! "What puzzles me is what your name has to do with being able to grow really big," he says. "I thought the names Mum gave us were supposed to be clues. At least Jacqueline with her jackal-in her makes sense. But *Albion?*"

"Let's save this until later," says Le Fay.

Albion, son of Neptune. Giant amongst men.

The next surprise is that Duffel has gotten hold of a car somewhere and has made some very basic conversions to it so that he can drive it (by adding blocks to the brake, clutch, and accelerator/gas pedals so that his short legs can reach them. That kind of thing). But the surprises don't end there. You'd probably get a bit of a shock if you were in a car—waiting at a traffic light, say—and you glanced across at the car next to you and saw that it's being driven by a teddy bear. So Duffel has gotten around this by wearing a disguise whenever he's out on the road, consisting of what looks like a yellow clown wig and a pair of women's dark glasses.

The car is hidden over on the other side of the disused bakery by a big roll-up/roll-down garage door. Duffel keeps the disguise on the backseat, so he leans in, takes it out, and puts it on: first the wig, then the glasses.

He's about to ask the McNallys what they think of it, but there's no need. Their reaction to his "new look" says it all. Fergal has his head thrown back and is howling; the twins are con-vulsed with laughter, hug-ging each other with glee; Le Fay is actually clutching her side—yes, clutching her  side—the laughter hurts so much and is pleading with him to "Take it off! Take it off!"; and even Jackie, who likes to be polite whenever possible and is doing her best *not* to laugh, has tears in her eyes.

"Okay, okay . . . ," says Duffel. "But can you drive, Jackie?" The others are too young to ask.

Jackie shakes her head. "I'm afraid not."

"Perhaps my secret power is to be a Formula One driver?" says Josh.

"I don't think we'll take a chance on that one!" says the teddy bear in the yellow wig and dark glasses. "Which means I'll have to drive—"

"—which means you'll have to wear the disguise—" says Albie.

"—and we'll have to try to stop laughing," says Josh.

"You've got it." Duffel nods. Truth be told, he doesn't mind the laughter one bit. They not only have a tough task ahead of them, but, if it works, he'll be going somewhere where there won't be much to laugh about.

"Everybody in," he says. "We must go and confront Doyle before he causes a rip to open up that does even more serious harm."

As he drives the McNallys out of town, on possibly their most unlikely exploit of all, Duffel tells them the name that Doyle is now using. He never expected the reaction is gets.

"*Medoc Silverman?*" says Jackie in amazement from the front passenger seat.

"Wasn't he the guy—"

"—at the Tap 'n' Type competition?" say the twins.

"Woof!" says Fergal (which is hardly surprising).

"He's Malcolm Kent's boss!" gasps Le Fay.

"You know him?" asks Duffel from under his wig and glasses.

"Not *know*, exactly," says Le Fay, "but his company sponsored a typing competition I won. He opened the grand finals. . . . That was the evening Fergal fell out of the window."

"That can't be a coincidence," says Duffel.

"How do you mean?" asks Jackie.

"I first saw you because, of all the brains Mulch could have stolen, he stole Fergal's from the Sacred Heart Hospital. That brought you into contact with me and Mr. Maggs, two of the three survivors who jumped through the Doughnut . . . but the fact that you'd also been in the presence of—in some way involved with—the third and only other survivor, Doyle-Silverman, too, surely means that it *can't* be a coincidence."

"Are you suggesting that this was somehow planned?" asks Le Fay, leaning forward, holding on to the back of Duffel's seat.

"Part of the great scheme of things?" says Duffel, his eyes on the road ahead. "Not exactly."

"Good," says Albie. "I don't like the idea of our having been born with these powers of ours for some—"

"—particular quest," adds Josh. "I never like stories with quests in them. They're always—"

"—the same, and always have people with names like Tharg, who speak—"

"—in riddles," says Josh. "And they always have very complicated plots. I don't like too much plot!"

"I was thinking more that the Laws of Nature might have a way of evening things out. If we play around with Time, treating the past like another country and coming visiting, Nature might find a way of redressing the balance."

"Undressing the what?" asks Albie.

"Putting things right," says Jackie.

"And you think that we might be a part of this not-exactly-great scheme of things?" asks Le Fay.

Fergal, who is on her lap in the back, breaks doggy wind. (That's a polite way of saying *f-a-r-t-s*.)

"Oh, Fergal!" groan the twins. "Smell-eeeee!" Josh rolls down a window.

"Woof!" says Fergal. *Sorry.*

"I'd like to think that putting right the Laws of Nature was left in better hands," Le Fay comments.

"I disagree," says Duffel. "Me, Smeek, and Doyle all decided to change our names—to take on new identities—but do you know how I ended up being called Duffel and Smeek became Mr. Maggs?"

"How?" asks Le Fay.

"Because those were the names *you* called us, Le Fay," says Duffel. "You met us both long before you ever came to Fishbone Hall."

Another time. Another place. Le Fay McNally is standing in a room. Much of it is in shadow. Something about the perspective seems a little strange: a little *off*. The walls don't quite meet the floor at right angles. The ceiling and the floor aren't quite parallel. Everything is shades of gray. The window—yes, there's a window, though she hadn't noticed it before—is not quite square. It's as though she's on some arty set in a black-and-white movie, a cross between a Salvador Dali painting and a 1950s cartoon that exaggerates and distorts everyday objects.

In a corner stands Smeek. His head is large, bald, and pumpkinlike since his hair fell out as a side effect of escaping through the Doughnut, most of it removed with a little help, and one big yank, from Doyle. His teeth are like shark's teeth. He looks up from whatever it is that he's doing.

"Who are you?" he asks in the familiar voice Le Fay thought that she'd never hear again.

"It's me, Le Fay McNally, Mr. Maggs," she says.

"What did you call me?" Smeek demands. *This is delicate work. How did she get in here?*

"Mr. Maggs," she repeats.

"And why do you call me that?" Smeek wonders. *Is she confusing me with someone else. And where's Doyle?*

"Because that's the name you insisted I call you," says Le Fay, stepping closer to him across the bare gray floorboards. "With the Mister and everything."

"When—?" begins Smeek. "Oh." His expression changes. "I think I understand." *I'm in a different time. A different place now. Maybe we've already met in a different future.*

"Mr. Maggs," says Smeek, slowly rolling the words around his mouth, trying out the new name for size. He grins in the shadows. "I like that. . . . You say we've met?"

"Yes," Le Fay nods. "In Fishbone Forest. I was the girl looking—er—for her dog. Don't you remember? You had a fall. . . . We all thought you were dead."

"And what was I doing in this Fishbone Forest?"

"You were planning to implement your *Manifesto of Change*. . . ." Le Fay is really close to him now.

Smeek smiles. "A manifesto of change? What an excellent idea. Our meeting like this is most fortuitous, Le Fay McNally. Really most fortuitous." *I like the idea of a manifesto,* thinks Smeek. *What kind of changes could I include in it? I'd change the order of the letters of the alphabet for a start!*

"How did you get out?" she asks.

"Out?"

"Of the hole?"

"Mr. Maggs . . . Fishbone Forest . . . *Manifesto of Change* . . . the hole," says Smeek. *By* hole *she must mean a rip caused by someone using the Doughnut. One day, I'll meet this girl Le Fay McNally again, and by then I'll be calling myself Mr. Maggs. What useful information.*

"I wish I understood what's happening," Le Fay says. "Everything is so strange."

Smeek stares intently into her eyes. *There's certainly something strange about you,* he muses. *How did you get here? What time are you from?* "You work it out," he says. *I must finish what I'm doing. Almost done.*

Le Fay looks down to see what he was working on when she came into the room. Her eyes widen. She screams. If this were a dream, she'd wake up now.

But this isn't a dream. There on the table lies a bloodied half man, half teddy bear.

"Duffel!" she cries.

ChAPTeR ELeven

"You're telling me that I was in the hut in the Australian desert where Smeek—Mr. Maggs—was putting you back together when you were still Carbonet . . . on the very day you all came through the Doughnut and ended up in 1993?" says Le Fay. "I think I'd remember that, don't you, Duffel?"

"But don't you see?" says the teddy bear, doing his best to concentrate on driving. "You haven't experienced that yet—it hasn't happened to *you* yet—but you will. It's in your future, but because you'll be going back to the past, the past has already been affected. That means that we're going to succeed in getting to use Doyle-Silverman's version of the Doughnut—"

"And that you knew we'd agree to help you before you even asked us," says Jackie, "because your knowing that Le Fay met Mr. Maggs before he ever ended up in Fishbone Forest means that she must get to use the time machine!"

Duffel nods. "Exactly," he says, "and if you're confused, don't worry about it. That's why we must put a stop to this time-travel business once and for all. It throws up too many inconsistencies, and the Laws of Nature, or the Laws of Physics or whatever you like to call them don't like inconsistencies."

"Hence the holes," says Le Fay.

"Hence the holes . . . another dangerous side effect."

"But there's a flaw in all of this!" Le Fay protests. "If, from Mr. Maggs's point of view, I'd already met him back in 1993, then why didn't he recognize me when we met again—from his perspective—in Fishbone Forest last year?"

"But he did," says Duffel. "He told me so."

"You're a long way from home, little one," says a voice in the gloom.

Le Fay looks up and gasps at the most extraordinary apparition standing before her. It is a man—at least, she assumes it's a man—clutching a huge teddy bear in one hand and a plastic orange tulip in the other. On top of his pumpkin-shaped head is a hat-cum-umbrella.

"I'm Mr. Maggs," he says softly, smiling a shark's-teeth smile. *It is you, isn't it, Le Fay McNally?* he's thinking. *You're the girl I met back in the shack, all that time ago, but no older. How can that be, I wonder?* "What brings you to my neck of the woods? This is private property. *Very* private property. You're trespassing on the Lyons family estate—well, *my* estate now, actually—little girl." *You somehow looked bigger back then,* he muses. *Still just a girl but more powerful, somehow. Not the bedraggled girl before me now.*

"I'm sorry, sir," says Le Fay ever so politely as her brain works overtime to come up with an excuse for being in Fishbone Forest.

"Mr. Maggs."

"I beg your pardon?" asks Le Fay.

"Call me Mr. Maggs." *When we met in the past, you were very clear how insistent I'd been on being called Mr. Maggs, so insistent I must be!*

"I'm sorry, *Mr. Maggs*," says Le Fay.

His mind is already racing. *When I first met you—back in the desert—you told me that I had a manifesto of change . . . and now I do, indeed, have one, Le Fay! I DO. I can hardly wait to tell you all about it!*

There is silence in the car until Le Fay finally breaks it. "So Mr. Maggs must have heard about Fishbone Forest from me too?"

"Yes."

"And found out about Lionel Lyons's fortune as a result?"

"Yes."

"And Fergal's brain only ended up in Bumbo's body because of his plans to put a brain in Mr. Lyons's body?"

"Yes," says Duffel.

"So, in a roundabout way, that's what saved Fergal!" Le Fay grins.

"I hadn't thought of that!" says Duffel, banging the steering wheel with a paw. "You're right! That proves what I said about there being no coincidences and the Laws of Nature wanting to balance things out! Doyle-Silverman indirectly brought about Fergal's death . . . and Smeek–Mr. Maggs indirectly brought about him coming back to life again. It's a balancing act!"

"Woof! Woof!" says Fergal. None of the others has any idea what he's just said, but he seems happy enough. He's got his head stuck out of the car window. The Bumbo blood pumping through his veins seems to be telling him that this is *just* the way that dogs like to travel.

On the outskirts of the capital is an area called Lockwood, full of very wide tree-lined streets—usually called something "Avenue"—with some very expensive houses sprawling across green lawns as neatly manicured as the best golf courses. Despite the spate of hot weather, which has left much of the rest of the country's grass parched and dry, these lawns are as green as a billiard/snooker/pool table's baize and as smooth. The loving care of privately employed gardeners, with the aid of thousands of gallons of water expelled by lawn sprinklers, has ensured that each lawn looks as perfect as the next.

Duffel brings his rather battered car to a halt at the curb next to the entrance to what little there is left of the woods from which the exclusive Lockwood suburb originally got its name.

"If we park this thing in front of any of the houses, it'll start the curtains twitching and we'll soon have a private security guard or policeman asking us what we're doing," Duffel explains. "If we cut through the woods, we come to the back of Doyle-Silverman's property on Cherry Tree Avenue."

"Does he have private security?" asks Le Fay.

The teddy bear nods. "But not people. Electronic. He has a whole system of alarms."

"And how are we going—"

"—to get past them—"

"—without triggering them?" ask the twins, climbing out of the car onto the pavement.

"They're key operated. If we enter the grounds through the main gate or the side gate, there's a key to deactivate the system," says Duffel. "I've tested it."

"You happen to have a key?" asks Jackie, stretching her legs. It's been a long drive.

"I do," says Duffel, still in his wig-and-glasses disguise. "Let's get under the cover of the trees before we attract any attention."

Fergal is reading a notice nailed to the trunk of a tree at the entrance to the woods.

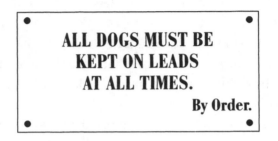

**ALL DOGS MUST BE
KEPT ON LEADS
AT ALL TIMES.**

By Order.

"Woof!" he says, pointing at it with his paw and then pointing at his neck.

Le Fay pulls the rolled-up leash out of her pocket and clips it to her brother's collar. "Well spotted," she says, giving him a pat.

In the shade of the trees—a cool relief after a journey in a car jam-packed with McNallys (some hairier than others)—Josh asks Duffel the obvious question: "How did you get your hands—"

"Paws."

"How did you get your paws on the key to Count Silverman's alarm system?"

"He kept a spare set hidden in his office in the Tap 'n' Type building. Very well hidden, in fact. They were taped to the underside of one of the drawers of his monstrous desk."

"So how did you find them?"

"Easy," he says. "By a fluke." (Funnily enough, *Fluke* is the title of a book by the horror writer James Herbert in which the hero finds himself reincarnated as a dog.) "Silverman stuffed me in a drawer when his secretary came into his office. I could see the set of keys taped to the bottom of the drawer above me."

"So you took them," says Le Fay.

"Yes," says Duffel, removing his disguise and handing the wig and glasses to her. "Could you carry these, please?" he asks. "I don't have any pockets."

"So where did you hide the keys, if you don't have any pockets?"

"I have a split in my side where the stuffing's coming out and my nerves and veins aren't connected up. I put them in there."

"So, even then, you suspected that Silverman-Doyle wouldn't cooperate and that the keys must be important to him or he wouldn't hide them in the first place?" says Le Fay.

They are moving down the path through the trees of all shapes and sizes (some of which have fared better in the weather than others). Being public property, no gardeners or sprinklers have been lavished on the woods.

"Of course," says Duffel. "Don't forget that I knew you would have to go back in time, to the shack where

Mr. Maggs saved my life, so I knew that I'd have to enlist your help."

"Something's been bothering me," says Jackie, stopping at the back of the group to free her leg from a tangle of brambles growing across the path. "The plan is to get you and the count, or Doyle, or whatever you like to call him, back through the Doughnut and then, I assume, you want us to destroy the machine so that no one else can use it and cause any holes?"

"That's right."

"So what's my sister doing going through it and ending up back in time?"

"Er." Duffel stops in his tracks. He turns to face her. "I have absolutely no idea."

"The more I think about this plan of yours, the less I like it," says Jackie.

"We've come this far," says Le Fay. "I say there's no turning back now . . . and then there's the matter of Fergal. If Duffel can get back to the time before he and the others escape through the Doughnut, then he can stop them from coming through and messing up time. There'll be no Tap 'n' Type, no competition, and Fergal will never fall out of that window. He'll be a human brain in a human body and none of this will ever have happened. Things will be back to how they should have been before a bunch of escaped prisoners"—she stops and looks at Duffel—"and an undercover government agent messed it up. Isn't that right?"

"It's a possibility," admits Duffel. "But I can't make any promises."

"And none of us will remember any of this because it won't have happened after all?" says Albie. "This is too weird."

These new thoughts fermenting in their minds, Duffel leads the McNallys off the path and to the western edge of the patch of woods, where there's a high wall. They follow it around until they reach a steel-reinforced door with an electronic box set into the brickwork next to it, with a large keyhole in it. A small red light is flashing.

"That means that the alarms to the grounds themselves are activated. They're on." Rather disconcertingly, the teddy bear puts his left paw through a split in the seam of his body and pulls out a small bunch of keys. He passes them to Le Fay. "You do it," he says. "I find it difficult to grasp with these paws." Le Fay takes the keys. "It's the big fat chrome one," he says. "I've checked the place out a few times."

Le Fay puts the key in the electronic box and turns. There's a tiny *bleep* and the red light stops flashing. She removes the key and is about to hand the bunch back to Duffel.

"No," he says. "Use the copper-colored one to open the gate, and then hang on to them for me."

Once inside the impressive grounds of Heyday— Count Silverman's rather strange choice of name for his home—they edge cautiously toward the house itself. This involves running across an area of lawn and then throwing themselves behind a tree . . . then running across another area of lawn and throwing themselves behind another tree . . . and so on. Fergal and Jackie (back in jackal form) act as scouts, slinking ahead on the lookout for anyone who might spot them. There's no sign of a gardener, security guard, anyone.

When they finally reach the house itself, they find a number of windows wide open to let in fresh air. It's obvious that someone is in the house and that the inner alarm must, therefore, be switched off. Le Fay holds out Jackie's clothes to her, and Jackie clenches them between her jackal teeth and disappears around the edge of the building, soon reemerging human shaped. It occurs to Le Fay that Albie's lucky his clothes grow to a giant size just as he does; otherwise he'd need a pair of those amazing stretching pants like the Incredible Hulk wears.

Following a request from Duffel, Josh gets onto Albie's shoulders, climbs through a window, and then opens a pair of French windows (glass doors) from the inside. The others now follow him into Heyday. Although they intend to confront Silverman, they need the element of surprise. With that in mind, they cautiously make their way around the house in search of him.

Chapter Twelve

For those of you expecting a picture at the beginning of this chapter, as with all the others, there's no time. We must get on! Silverman, Doyle—call him what you will—is in his workshop when the McNallys burst through the door. They want the element of surprise on their side, and that's what they've got.

A jackal once more, Jackie comes in first, snarling and behaving in as generally a frightening way as any jackal can without actually biting anybody. Her hackles are up—in other words, her fur is sticking out—and her teeth are bared. She is snarling and has her eyes on Count Silverman and Silverman alone.

Next comes Fergal. Now, I'm a big lover of mongrel dogs, but even if you're not, I'm sure you'll agree from the illustrations that he's pretty c-u-t-e. But as most of you know, even the cutest dog can be a bit frightening when it wants to be. With his teeth bared and making his own snarly noises, he too seems far from friendly and, in conjunction with his big sister, does the four-legged contingency of the Duffel-McNally attack team proud.

Next come Duffel and Le Fay, side by side and ready for business. Theirs is a different kind of surprise. The count wasn't expecting to see Duffel again so soon and Le Fay McNally ever. *Isn't she the girl who won the typing competition last year???*

"What is this?" demands Silverman. "What's going on here?" He looks frantically about for something to defend himself against the jackal—yes, that's a jackal, all right, he knows his animals—and the dog, and the others. Like his office at Tap 'n' Type, the walls of his workshop are covered with gold musical instruments, none of which would make a particularly good weapon. He resorts to the contents of his toolbox and wields the biggest screwdriver he can find. "Stay back!" he says, taking a step back himself. "Don't come any nearer."

Now the last two remaining McNallys enter the room: the twins, Albie and Josh, looking as harmless as a pair of cuddly bunnies.

"Ha!" says Silverman with a wild look in his eye, singular (more on that in a moment). "It's Tweedledum and Tweedledee!"

In that instant, Albie thinks big, as planned, and grows into his giant self, the rumbling that this causes echoing around the workshop. Silverman looks on in complete and utter disbelief, tilting his head back to watch the boy grow. He drops the screwdriver in amazement.

Fergal bounds forward and picks it up in his mouth.

Jackie-the-jackal launches herself at the stunned Silverman, who stumbles back onto the small stool he was sitting on when tinkering with his machine before their dramatic entrance. Jackie stands guard only inches in front of him. All the fight appears to have gone out of him.

Now they have a chance to take in their surroundings. This is the first time the McNallys have seen any of the Doughnuts, and it's certainly impressive. As for Count Medoc Silverman, he's not like the Count Medoc Silverman the McNallys saw on stage at The Dell hotel at the Tap 'n' Type grand finals last winter, and he's not like the Count Medoc Silverman whom Duffel confronted much more recently at his office. His usually immaculate pinstriped suit is tattered and torn and he's wearing an eye patch—yup, an eye patch—over his right eye.

"You've come to take us back, haven't you, Carbonet?" he says to Duffel, his shoulders sagging and his voice more of a moan.

"Yes," says Duffel. "Even if we find we can't put right the damage we've done by coming to this time, at least we'll stop making it worse. . . . We'll stop changing more history."

"But I don't want to go back!" says the count, by which, of course, he means going forward to the future they come from.

Duffel looks around at his ragbag army of . . . of, well, *McNallys*. "We're not here to give you a choice but to make sure you go."

"But there's a glitch with my Doughnut," says Silverman. "Look at me. Look what it's done." He certainly looks the worse for wear.

"You've been through the machine?" asks Josh. "But how could you have been? I mean, you'd have needed *another* machine to go through to get back here."

"I set the coordinates for this room but a week ago. I simply came back through this machine when it was a week younger," sighs Silverman.

"AMAZING!" says—you guessed it—big, big Albion. He's staying enormous to make sure that the count stays intimidated.

"And it did this to you?" says Duffel.

"Yes," says Silverman. "It felt like being stung by a giant jellyfish or grated by a giant cheese grater. I-I've lost an eye." He lifts the eye patch to reveal a very raw and unpleasant wound. "You can't take me through there, Carbonet! You could be killing the both of us."

Le Fay is studying the huge metal ring, much of it made from gold. "If you can be precise enough to send yourself back to this very place but a week before, you must be able to set the coordinates to send yourself to the prison at the precise time and place before you first escaped," she says.

"It's too risky, I tell you! Too risky!" whines Silverman, and, before anyone realizes quite what's happening, he's leapt to his feet and is giving Le Fay a desperate shove. She falls backward through the hole in the Doughnut. He slams the flat palm of his hand against the control pad . . . and she disappears.

"WHAT HAVE YOU DONE?" roars Albie.

Le Fay is falling, falling, falling. She is witnessing a whole variety of events—some familiar, some new, some half-forgotten memories reawakened—all around her. She's a part of them, intimately involved in all of them, yet at the same time is somehow distant from them: an observer. There she is in the shack with Mr. Maggs . . . with the twins in the park . . . in the first round of the typing competition . . . crying alone in a room . . . being given a piggyback by Jackie. . . . This is nothing like Duffel had described so-called time travel would be!

Of course it isn't, says a voice. Her own voice? It certainly sounds familiar.

Not your voice. My voice.

It is the voice of the fortune-teller she heard at Wanda-
land before venturing into Fishbone Forest last winter. It
is the voice of—

Yes, darling. I am your mother.

Mum? But you're dead.

*Am dead. Was dead. Will be dead. We are all these things at some
time or other, my sweetheart.*

What's going on, Mum?

You're out of Time, Le Fay.

You mean I'm about to die too?

*No, you're standing outside time. Few can do it. You are one of the
few. I named you after Morgan Le Fay, my clever daughter. Morgan*

Le Fay was sister to King Arthur. Some called her a sorceress. Some a magician, but these are just titles . . . labels . . . words. She held the secrets to some of the most important magic. She was one of the most powerful people to walk the earth. So will you be, Le Fay.

Does that mean that I can put things right? That I can stop Fergal falling from the window—

What you can do and should do are not necessarily the same thing. Sometimes what's done is done and should remain so. Aren't you and dear Rufus now happier than you've ever been, Le Fay?

If we're outside time, Mum, what's that ticking?

It's clicking, not ticking.

Clicking?

Of knitting needles.

You're knitting at a time like this?

Yes, two pairs of booties. And we're OUT of Time, remember?

Your voice is fading, Mum! says Le Fay. Don't go! Please don't go!

Remember this above all, cries her mother. *No kind deed is ever wasted.*

"Mum!" Le Fay calls out loud. "Mum! We all love you! Me, Jackie, the twins. Even little Fergal, who never really knew you. We all love you!" She's shouting now as she spirals past more and more events in her life, slightly distorted and washed of color.

"I know!" Freya McNally calls back and, in that brief moment, Le Fay can actually see her. Unlike everything around her, she is really there: she is solid flesh and bone, sitting in a simple room of brilliant light, with a huge pair of knitting needles. "I'm so proud of you all!"

Then there is a loud belching—yup, the deep wet kind—and Le Fay finds herself tumbling out of the Doughnut onto the floor of Silverman's workshop.

"See?" says Silverman, who is lying on the floor, hands tied behind his back with his own tie, with Jackie-the-jackal and Fergal sitting on his chest and stomach. "It's not working!" Fergal jumps off him and bounds over to Le Fay, jumping up at her in excitement at her safe return, his tail wagging excitedly.

The twins (both small and almost identical) run forward. "Are you okay, Le Fay?"

"I'm . . . I'm fine," says Le Fay.

"You look different," says Josh. "Bigger, somehow."

"Powerful!" says Albie. "That's what it is. . . . What happened to you?"

"I discovered my secret power," she says. "I'll explain later. Right now there's work to be done." She turns to Duffel, who is punching codes into the keypad on the Doughnut.

"Take Doyle back to your own time, Duffel, but don't try to put right what you've done to this one. That's our history now. It's happened, so you could just end up making things worse. . . . By changing history, you've already changed the future. . . . What you go back to won't be the same as the future you escaped from anyway," she says. "Who knows what you might find."

"This really is a mess, isn't it?" says Duffel. "What happened to you in there?"

"I'm just a kid." She shrugs. "What do I know?"

The teddy bear stares at the small freckle-faced girl with the wiry red hair and the gappy teeth. "A lot more than you'll ever tell, Le Fay," he says. "I always knew that you were the right ones to come to." He turns to Silverman. "Come on, Doyle. We've got an important appointment to keep." The others help the disheveled count to his feet. Jackie takes the opportunity to nip behind a workbench and soon reappears as a fully dressed sister.

Duffel punches in a final code and the Doughnut begins to hum again.

"Well, good-bye, everybody," he says. "Thank you. . . ." He pauses. "And please try not to think too badly of any of us. We were in the wrong place at the wrong time, that's all. . . . Come on, Doyle."

Count Medoc Silverman has his eyes downcast. He won't look at them. "I'm sorry . . . ," he says. Together they step into the ring and are gone.

"Good-bye, Duffel," says Le Fay in almost a whisper, knowing that it is too late for him to hear the words anyway. "Good luck."

"Now what?" asks Jackie.

"We destroy this thing before it does any more damage. Somewhere some new holes will already have opened up because we just used it."

"Shall I grow to my giant size and stamp on it?" asks Albie eagerly.

"Woof," says Fergal. *Great idea.*

"No, we'll let Josh do it," says Le Fay.

"Woof?" says Fergal. *How come?*

"Because I know his secret—"

"You can understand Fergal's barks!" Jackie interrupts.

"Oh yes," says Le Fay, surprised. "I suppose I can. . . . Now that I know my power, it's been unlocked."

"You can talk to animals?" asks Albie.

"You know *my* power?" asks Josh excitedly.

"Oh yes," says Le Fay. She knows most things now. She is most powerful, whatever label you may choose to give her.

"What is it? What is it?"

Le Fay dashes over to the nearest wall and pulls a beautiful gold trumpet from its brackets, just one of the many instruments lining the room. "Take this," she says. "And everybody out. Hurry. We must destroy the machine right now."

They leave the workshop and hurry out into the garden.

"Blow," says Le Fay.

"What?" asks Josh.

"Blow that trumpet," says Le Fay.

Josh puts the mouthpiece of the trumpet to his lips and blows. A fantastically loud note blasts out of the instrument.

"You're a natural!" Le Fay laughs. "Play us a tune."

"But I don't know how—" Josh protests.

"Just do it!" says Le Fay.

And Josh starts playing. Brilliantly. And loudly. And the ground starts to tremble and the house starts to rumble and shake.

"I think we should run!" says Jackie, and everyone takes a big sister's advice. They've just reached the gate through to the woods when Silverman's house collapses in a pile of rubble. All eyes are on the twin.

"Nice one, Josh," says Le Fay. "It seems Mum named you after Joshua in the Bible. The Joshua who ordered his army to blow trumpets that led to the collapse of the walls of Jericho. I think you'll find that you can play just about any instrument and each will have a different effect!"

"Like I can charm snakes and . . . and . . . ?"

"And that kind of thing." Le Fay nods.

"Cooooool, brother!" says Albie. Josh can't wait to put his newfound talents to the test.

Le Fay unlocks the gate and they pile out into the woods. As they walk down the path back toward the car, Jackie has a worrying thought. "Uh-oh! I think we're in a bit of a fix," she says.

"What do you mean?" says Le Fay.

"We never thought about how we'd get back home! We don't have Duffel to drive us!"

Le Fay gives her a toothy grin. "No problem, Jacks. I'll drive."

"You can drive all of a sudden?" asks Jackie as they all clamber into the car.

Le Fay gets into the driver's seat. "I can do lots of things now."

There are people in the street dashing here, there, and everywhere as a result of the collapse of the house on Cherry Tree Avenue. No one is giving the out-of-place McNallys a second glance.

"The emergency services are on their way!" one neighbor shouts to another.

"I'll bet it was one of those holes," a third neighbor speculates. "Opened right up under the count's house!"

The McNallys know better, of course. They've put an end to the holes.

There's a wail of distant sirens.

Le Fay turns the key in the ignition and the car engine comes to life.

"Wait a minute!" says Albie. "You're just a kid. We could be pulled over by the police."

"You don't mean?" says Le Fay hesitantly.

"Yup!" says Josh. "You must—"

"PUT ON THE DISGUISE!" they shout as one, followed by fits of laughter and barking.

Le Fay reaches for the wig and glasses in her pocket.

Chapter Thirteen

Now our final leap forward. Not a big one. There, it's done. At last Lionel Lyons's money is being used the way the real Lionel Lyons would have wanted it to have been: helping others. Tom Dwyer, now the brains inside his body, is ensuring that the huge fortune is put to very good use indeed, as described in the wishes expressed in Lionel's writings, first jotted down as an eight-year-old after that little talk his father gave him on his knee. And do you know what? It's made Dwyer a happy man too. For him, helping others beats teaching French any day.

With the able and unique assistance of the McNally siblings—bound to him by their knowledge of his secret and his of theirs—the money not only goes to help the big causes (famine relief, war aid, and the fight against disease, for example) but also to help the small individual causes that can make such a difference (a teddy bear for a child who's never had one, a pet for an old people's home, a vacation for those who've never been away from home before, help for an injured badger). I'm sure you can think of examples of your own.

Charlie "Twinkle-Toes" Tweedy has proved very useful in tracking down worthy recipients, and Malcolm Kent is excellent at publicizing the work of the charity. People have been helped far and wide, but, as Jackie pointed out, "charity begins at home."

Noble drives a breakdown truck for a living. He enjoys his work because he likes helping people, and most motorists are very glad to see a breakdown truck if their car won't go and they're stuck at the side of the road. He has a big oily toolbox in the back of the truck and will only tow a car away if he fails to fix the problem at the roadside or if the car is beyond repair.

Noble's head looks a lot like a large turnip, and, if you don't know what a turnip is, it's a big round root vegetable that looks a lot like Noble's head. I'm not being rude. Noble is the first to admit that he's "no oil painting." But what does he care? He loves his job. He loves his wife and three boys, and they love him right back.

If you were to ask Noble about some of the most significant events in his life, he's unlikely to include the time he gave a ride to four members of the McNally family last winter. Sure, he remembers it. Who wouldn't? You don't see two almost-identical twins every day, nor a boy (Fergal) dressed in a diaper, just so that he'd been able to travel on a bus free of charge. And then there'd been the young woman who was with them, their big sister Jackie. She'd been most appreciative of his driving them into town and dropping them off near The Dell hotel, where, Noble strongly suspects, they were planning to stay *w-i-t-h-o-u-t p-a-y-i-n-g*.

But would Noble have seen giving the McNallys a ride in his breakdown truck as a truly significant event? Most probably not. The significant events in Noble's life were when he first laid eyes on the future Mrs. Noble (who was called Maggie Jupp back then) across a crowded pigpen on her father's farm, or the day he married her, or the days when each of their boys—Pug, Gamble, and Benjy—was born. That kind of thing. Giving the McNallys a ride up in the cab of his truck has been just one of Noble's many acts of kindness. Which just goes to show, you never know where a good deed might lead.

Wednesday morning begins like any other Wednesday morning in the Noble family, but then the oldest son, Pug, pulls open the curtains in his bedroom and sees what is out in the yard. Soon everyone is outside except for Noble himself, who, blissfully unaware that anything is out of the ordinary, is in the bathroom going through his morning routine. He's had his bath and washed his hair and is in the process of shaving when he hears a cry.

"Dad!" Benjy, the youngest, shouts up to Noble from the bottom of the stairs. "Daaaaaaaaad!" Assuming that if it is *that* important, then Benjy will come upstairs and tell him what he wants, Noble chooses to ignore his youngest.

"Daaaaaaaaaaaaaaaaaaad!" Benjy shouts again, *really* loudly this time.

Noble, who is shaving with an old straight-edge razor in front of the cracked bathroom mirror, carefully runs the blade under the tap and folds it shut. "What is it, Benjy!" he asks, emerging onto the landing.

"Come look!" says Benjy. "Come quick."

Noble can hear the excitement in the boy's voice. He sounds like he does on Christmas morning. Noble runs grinning down the stairs two at a time, his face still covered with foam. "What is it, Benjy?" he repeats, now clearly intrigued.

Benjy grabs his dad's wrist and pulls him—leads him, more like—through the kitchen, past the pantry office, out through the open back door, and into the yard.

Noble stops and stares.

STOPS and STARES.

There.

Slow down.

This is a big moment.

You read about people's eyes opening wide in amazement. You read about people's jaws dropping. Well, the eyes in Noble's turniplike head don't get any wider. The jaw of his turniplike head doesn't drop. He simply stops and stares.

There in his backyard, next to the old and battered breakdown truck he's had for many, many years, is a brand-spanking-new one. It is bigger. It is better. And there down the side, in gleaming red letters outlined in gold, are the words: **NOBLE'S BREAKDOWNS**, which are the very words he hand-painted (rather badly) on his old truck many years before.

On the top of the cab of the truck is an enormous red bow, reminding Noble of a helicopter rotor blade. (He sometimes helps out at Fairwick Airport and has even worked on a helicopter engine.) In the truck sit Pug and their middle son, Gamble. Pug is at the steering wheel, pretending to drive. He sees Noble come outside. "This is great, Dad!"

"Brilliant!" agrees Gamble at his side. He does a big thumbs-up.

Still clutching his father's wrist, Benjy is jumping up and down in uncontrollable excitement. "See!" he shouts. "See!"

Noble walks over to his wife, who is staring at the new truck in disbelief. He puts his arm around her shoulders. "It's beautiful, Jon," she says. "But where did it come from?"

"I don't know," Noble confesses. His mind is already racing ahead with possibilities. Is this really for him?

It has **NOBLE'S BREAKDOWNS** on the side.

It *must* be.

Has Maggie finally won the state lottery after all these years of trying and is simply pretending not to know where the truck came from?

His mind is really racing. With *two* trucks he could handle twice as much work if he hires a second driver. Bob Lesley. That's it! He could hire his friend Bob Lesley to drive the other one. Bob isn't much of a mechanic since he had his accident and lost his job, but Noble could send him out to tow away the car wrecks that are beyond repair. He could pay Bob's wages out of the extra money the extra work would bring in. That'd be good: more work for Noble's Breakdowns and a job for Bob . . . if this truck is somehow really his.

Noble walks over to the cab, climbs onto the running board, and pulls open the driver's door. "Shift over, boys," he says, and they shunt along the bench seat so that their dad can sit behind the wheel.

"Me! Me!" Benjy shouts from the ground, and his mother passes him up to Noble, who sits him on his knee.

"This was in the glove compartment, Dad," says Gamble, passing Noble a gold envelope.

Noble tears it open.

"This is like one of those award ceremonies on TV," says Pug. "And the winner is . . ."

"Whassit say? Whassit say?" demands Benjy, looking at the card his father is pulling from the envelope. (He is too young to read.)

No kind deed is ever wasted.

Noble reads out the words.

"Who's it from, Jon?" asks Maggie Noble.

He passes her down the card through the open cab door. "I've no idea, love," he says. "Does that lion symbol at the bottom mean anything to you?"

Mrs. Noble digs her hand in her apron pocket and pulls out a pair of old black-framed reading glasses, which she proceeds to perch on the end of her nose and squint through at the card. She makes a face. "Nothing," she says. "Do you really think this truck is ours to keep?"

"I most certainly do," says Noble. He's found what else is in the envelope: all the ownership, tax, insurance, and registration documents required in this particular country at this particular time to show that the brand-spanking-new breakdown truck belongs to Mr. Jon Noble and is licensed to drive on the roads.

Noble lifts Benjy off his lap and steps back out onto the running board, placing him directly in front of the steering wheel. Benjy whoops with joy and grabs it with both hands, making engine noises.

Noble jumps to the ground with a crunch of gravel and hugs and kisses his wife. When they finally let go of each other, both of them seem to have shaving-foam beards.

Hidden by a nearby bush, a dog watches the delighted Nobles circling their new truck. He has a lolling tongue and a happy expression on his face. His tail bangs on the ground with obvious delight. If I had to attribute human emotions to him, I'd suggest that he might be thinking: *Mission accomplished. A job well done.*

He turns and heads for home, where his loving and happy family is waiting for him.

THE END
of this, the final exploit

EPILOGUE

Dear Ralphie,

Thank you for the human brain. It was much more suitable than the juvenile brain my idiot assistant provided for the task, and was a perfect fit.

I'm so glad you made it through the Doughnut before my arrest.

Here's hoping we can get together sometime.

Your loving cousin,

"Maggs"

ABOUT THE AUTHOR

Over six feet seven inches tall, with a bushy beard, there's no doubt that Philip Ardagh is not only very big but also very hairy. He writes fiction and nonfiction for all ages, and the books in his Eddie Dickens Trilogy are bestsellers.

When not writing silly books, Philip Ardagh is very serious indeed and frowns a great deal. He lives in a sea-side town somewhere in England with his wife and their son, Fred. He used to have two cats, and misses them both very much.

www.philipardaghbooks.com